A Vineyard Wedding

The Vineyard Sunset Series

Katie Winters

ALL RIGHTS RESERVED. No part of this publication may be reproduced, distributed, or transmitted in any form or by any means, including photocopying, recording, or other electronic or mechanical methods, without the prior written permission of the publisher.

Copyright © 2020 by Katie Winters

This is a work of fiction. Any resemblance of characters to actual persons, living or dead is purely coincidental. Katie Winters holds exclusive rights to this work. Unauthorized duplication is prohibited.

Chapter One

Susan Sheridan's long-ago days at the law offices of Harris and Harris, back in Newark, New Jersey, had little to do with her current role as the head criminal defense attorney at the Sheridan Law Offices located in Oak Bluffs on Martha's Vineyard. For one: Richard Harris, her now ex-husband, was no longer a dominating force, and she found that she liked to run a very different kind of ship— one that focused far more on compassion than on manipulation, volatility, and rage. She and Richard had been regarded as some of the best criminal defense attorneys on the east coast, but already, there in the newly opened Sheridan Law Offices, Susan had crafted another reputation. "She has heart," someone had described on a social media review. "Not that anyone who isn't the daughter of Wes and Anna Sheridan wouldn't have heart."

It thrilled Susan to work in law again, and it made her pulse race with excitement as she received each new case. Prior to this, her eight or so months as the operating manager of the Sunrise Cove Inn had been beautiful. She'd manned the very desk her father and mother had shared all those years ago and watched with an earnest eye as Scott and other craftsmen had built the place back up to its former glory. But with the newly hired Sam at the front desk, along with Natalie and the rest of the staff, the Sunrise Cove didn't need Susan's ever-watchful eye.

Susan was allowed the best of both worlds: her beloved family and her second true love, law— a space where her creativity and attention to detail flourished. The fact that her daughter, Amanda, had wanted to join forces with her, even as she continued on at law school at Rutgers, thrilled her all the more. Perhaps they would operate as business partners for many years together. It was beyond her wildest dreams— especially as she had thought she would have to say goodbye to Amanda for "good" after her marriage to Chris.

In a sense, Chris's dastardly dash from the wedding altar was a blessing in hindsight. Although who in their right mind left a girl like Amanda? It stumped Susan to think about it.

Susan stepped up from her desk and reached her arms over her head. Her mind buzzed with the events of the day. It had been a standard set of events which included a brief meeting with Jennifer Conrad, who had wanted to solidify a few of the legalities surrounding her social media management company, then a brief meeting with Claire and Russell, who had discussed the last-minute details of Russell's case, which had found him accused of stealing a number of funds from the city of Oak Bluffs. The poor guy hadn't known what to do with himself in the wake of those accusations.

A Vineyard Wedding

The foyer of the Sheridan Law Office was empty and echoing. "Amanda?" Susan tried as she furrowed her brow. Ordinarily, from this view, the top of Amanda's perfectly shining head of beautiful hair hovered over the top of the foyer desk as she scribbled notes to herself. Susan stepped toward it and discovered one of Amanda's classic to-do notes.

1. Manage the files for the Casey case.
2. Type the notes from yesterday's meeting.
3. Pilates???
4. Ice cream with Sam.
5. Wedding dress shopping with Mom!

Ah! Of course. Susan beamed at the paper as she stepped back. Throughout the previous months, Amanda and the front desk manager at the Sunrise Cove had built a flourishing friendship. Light danced in Amanda's eyes when he came up in conversation. Probably, it was still too soon after Amanda's four-year relationship and failed engagement for her to fall into anything serious. Even still, Susan felt the buds of whatever was next for them; it was as though they operated under the belief that the future was theirs. They would simply enjoy the journey without rushing it.

And oh yes. Susan had nearly forgotten that she'd agreed to meet Amanda, Christine, Lola, and Audrey at the wedding dress shop in Edgartown. She lifted her wrist to check the time and realized she only had a little over an hour before she needed to head out.

There was a volatile creak from the door. Susan's eyes lifted as a large man of maybe six foot five inches burst through the door. He wore all black— a black leather jacket and black jeans, and his hair was puffy and wild, with a huge patch on top where he'd lost some. It seemed he hadn't smiled in maybe ten years. He looked to be around fifty, with crow's feet at the corners of his eyes, along with his hardened frown lines and wrinkles, suggesting that this man was under a lot of stress and very saddened by something. Susan had never seen him before.

"Good afternoon! Did you have an appointment with us?" Susan knew for a fact that they didn't have any more appointments for the day. Amanda wouldn't have left before the last one.

The man grunted. He pushed his hands into his pockets and looked at Susan with disdain. Susan had never felt in danger on the island, but this man sent a chill up and down her spine.

"I can make an appointment for you later in the week," Susan continued. "If you'd like. Just let me check the book—"

"I don't have an appointment," the man grumbled. "But I need to speak with you. It's extremely urgent."

Something about his voice stopped Susan in her tracks. She blinked up at him, aghast, then dropped her hands to her sides.

"You are Susan Sheridan, correct?"

Susan nodded. "I am."

"I've heard you're the best criminal defense lawyer in the area. Not just on this godforsaken island. And I need your help."

There was an urgency behind the man's voice; the light behind his eyes was dark green and strange. Susan walked back and opened the door to her office even more. Fear wasn't an option for her. In fact, in her many years of work in criminal defense, she'd sat across from murderers, thieves and other reckless criminals; she'd learned to deal with the fear and brush it aside.

After all, Susan was often these criminals' last hope at a normal life. Regardless if they had committed the crimes or not, regardless of the evil that lurked within their soul— she had to be a human for them. She couldn't judge them. She could only use the law to serve them.

"Please. Sit. Can I get you some water? A cup of coffee?"

The man shook his head. He dropped down into the chair across from Susan and studied his hands, which were massive and covered with dark, thick hair. Susan waited in silence for the man to start speaking as it did no good for her to press him for information. He'd come for a reason, and he would soon reveal it.

"You've probably heard of my daughter," he said finally. "Marcie Shean."

Something in the back of Susan's mind rang like a bell. She clicked her pen and wrote the name out on a yellow pad of paper.

"Marcie grew up here on the island. Like you. Like me," the man continued. "But she left the island at age twenty to make a new life for herself up in Boston. We lost touch for a few years. We never had— well. We never had the best relationship, but she came back sometimes to see her younger brother. He's still in high school. Their mom died in childbirth with our second, so she's been gone a long time."

Susan's heart dropped just the slightest bit. She did her best to maintain a stoic expression.

"Marcie's twenty-five, now. And I guess you must have heard what happened. Last November, up in Boston — well, her boyfriend, Freddy, died. Actually, he was murdered. Marcie is the one who found him, but apparently, there was evidence at the scene to suggest otherwise," he said, palming the back of his neck.

Susan had long since understood that parents took a tremendous toll when their children were accused of murder. It stood to reason. If Jake or Amanda had ever gotten into any trouble, she had always thought she could handle it, just as she'd handled everything else. But in all honesty, it touched on a dark part of her heart that made her not-so-sure.

"Is she still up in Boston?" Susan asked.

The father shook his head. "No. They allowed her to come home, to stay with me on house arrest." He sniffed and smeared a finger beneath his nostrils. "Marcie and I don't always see eye to eye, Mrs. Sheridan, but I know she isn't a murderer."

"You said the crime happened in November?"

"But the trial starts up in two weeks," the man continued. "I don't know what to do about it. We had a lawyer all lined up— a damn good one out of Boston, but just last week, after all the jury had been selected and everything, he dropped Marcie's file. He explained it was something to do with his wife and an illness. It doesn't matter. The only thing that does is that we need a new lawyer now. And I hope that lawyer will be you."

Fascination made Susan's heart swell. She squeezed her knee beneath the desk and pictured herself again in a large-scale court, fully prepared to represent a high-profile client, a woman who was wanted for the murder of her boyfriend. Of course, she had pity for the girl and for the boy's family. But beyond that, she hadn't been able to sink her teeth into a case like this in years.

"I'll need to meet with your daughter as soon as possible," Susan told him, leaning into the desk. "If the trial is set to begin in two weeks, I don't have much time to build a case."

The man's eyes widened just the slightest bit. "Does this mean you'll take us on?"

Susan nodded as she lifted her pen again toward the pad of paper. "Can you give me the details for your previous lawyer? He'll need to forward any and all case files to my office immediately."

The man drew his wallet out of his back pocket. The wallet seemed sticky; the cards within, which he dragged out onto the surface of her desk, seemed to have collected stains from various soda pops and spilled waters. Finally, he found the lawyer's business card and placed it in front of Susan. The font was hardly legible; Susan could just barely make out the name and email address of the guy.

"You don't know what this means to us. To me," the father said as he stood. Again, he looked overly tall for his body— as though he had been stretched beyond what was naturally allowed. He placed his wallet back in his pocket and blinked down at Susan.

"I just need you to fill out a few forms for me, if that's okay," Susan said. "Email address, your phone number, your address— that kind of thing. It will give me the basics for my files."

The man nodded and accepted the clipboard, which he took out into the foyer. Probably, he wanted to avoid even more conversation with Susan.

This was all the better for Susan, as she wanted to dive fully into the world of Marcie Shean and this heinous crime that she was being accused of. At this point, with very little information to go off of, Susan felt like a blind woman headed into a burning building. It thrilled her and terrified her at the same time.

She knew one thing for sure: over the next few weeks, she would have a lot on her plate. Everything else would play second-fiddle.

Chapter Two

After Marcie's father, Ralph, departed for the evening, Susan rapped her nails hurriedly over her keyboard and drew up the bright-eyed face of Marcie Shean— a truly beautiful blond girl whose emerald eyes illuminated from the front page of the Boston newspaper back in November.

BOSTON BEAUTY ACCUSED OF SLAYING BOYFRIEND

In the photo, Marcie's hands were latched behind her back as cops yanked her toward the cop car. She looked directly into the camera as though someone had just called her name. In a moment of weakness, or in thinking that the name-calling was friendly, she'd turned for solace. In return, she'd gotten only the flash of a camera.

One of the articles came up with a description of what was currently known about the case. Susan placed her reading glasses on the tip of her nose and drew her face toward the screen. Outside, the light dimmed toward evening.

Although Susan knew clearly not to rely on the

internet or any articles fully, she still read, and here is what Susan learned through this cursory read-through:

Marcie Shean and boyfriend Vincent Camden met three months after Marcie arrived in Boston, after her departure from Martha's Vineyard at the age of twenty. They met when Marcie worked as a hostess at a high-scale restaurant, and Vincent worked as one of the bartenders. According to many eyewitnesses and colleagues, the pair was inseparable almost immediately. They moved in with one another approximately six months after their initial meeting into a house in South End, Boston, which was largely known as a dangerous neighborhood.

The years after that cast Marcie and Vincent toward other jobs. Marcie had brief stints at universities but always dropped out due to money problems. According to many newspapers, Marcie kept her distance from her roots on Martha's Vineyard, while Vincent had had minor contact with his mother and father, who lived just outside of Boston, in Manchester-by-the-Sea, which was a very small town.

According to several reports, Vincent's parents had never really taken to Marcie. They thought she was too young for their son (only five years between the two), and they also blamed her for Vincent's constant partying—which didn't seem fair to Susan, as it seemed that Vincent had long since been involved in the party scene of Boston, especially since he'd worked as a bartender.

According to several friends of the couple, Vincent and Marcie had recently had plenty of relationship troubles. Naturally, they hadn't been able to afford any form of therapy, and they'd taken to screaming at one another with all the windows open. Even when the windows were

A Vineyard Wedding

closed, neighbors reported feeling fearful that the two might rip into one another. Of course, they'd said this only after the murder itself— which made it difficult to know what they'd actually thought during the fights themselves. Young couples fought, especially as they grew into themselves and tried to assess if this was the relationship they wanted for the rest of their days. Everyone knew that.

According to Marcie's reports, Marcie arrived home from a trip to the grocery store to find Vincent stabbed to death in their kitchen. It had been a complete surprise to her; it had ripped her two. She'd called 911 immediately and apparently, when they had arrived, they'd found that she'd fallen to the ground at Vincent's side, holding him.

But there were also fingerprints all over the murder weapon, and those fingerprints belonged to Marcie Shean herself.

Susan's heart raced as she glanced back at this poor girl's face. Did she have the capacity to do something like this? Susan had certainly worked with a number of female criminals. No, they didn't normally look so angelic, but many of them had had feminine elements; they'd sang sweetly and loved deeply and batted their eyelashes just so. Susan knew better than to trust a wolf in sheep's clothing.

Still, there on the front page of the newspaper, Susan saw a terrified girl— a girl who had lost someone she'd once loved in cold blood. Susan shook strangely with the adrenaline of it all.

Suddenly, she realized that her office had dimmed to a strange gray. She yanked herself around to catch sight of the sun as it dropped toward the western end of Oak

Bluffs. With a jolt, she grabbed her phone and found it filled with calls and messages, all from Amanda.

> AMANDA: Mom! Where are you?
>
> AMANDA: Pick! Up! Your! Phone!
>
> AMANDA: Nobody else is here, anyway. What is it with this family? Why am I the only one who arrives anywhere on time?

Susan flung the phone to her ear as it rang twice. "Hey! Amanda!"

"Mom! What happened? You're twenty-five minutes late."

"I know. I'm running to the car right now. I'll be there so fast that you won't even notice."

Amanda groaned as Susan turned off the lights in the office and fled out into the soft light of an early evening in May. It had now been about a year since Susan had arrived on the island, and her stomach panged with nostalgia. When she'd first arrived, she couldn't have imagined even a tenth of all that had happened.

Now, she had built up her career again after leaving her old firm; she was engaged to marry the original love of her life, and she was closer to her sisters and her father more than ever before. And this was all just the beginning.

When Susan rushed into the Edgartown wedding dress shop, she found Amanda on the sofa, her brow furrowed. She stretched her arms out on either side of her and said, "See? Still, nobody here. I don't know what you Sheridan girls think about other people's time, but..."

Susan groaned and tossed herself on the couch alongside Amanda. "I'm here now, aren't I?"

"Yes, but Mom. Look at this list." Amanda yanked a pad of paper from her purse and waved it around. "It's crazy the number of things we still have to get done for your wedding. You know, it's only six weeks away?"

"I'm well aware of that."

"And we still don't have a dress, and we haven't solidified the menu, and we haven't even checked on all the invitations..."

"Amanda. I'm here now. Okay?" she said, placing a hand on her daughter's arm to calm her.

Amanda closed her eyes and heaved a sigh. It had always been this way with Amanda. Sometimes, she got so locked in her head, in the way "things had to be," that she struggled to see the big picture. Susan longed to tell her that she would wear a paper bag as a dress if she had to. The only thing that mattered to her was that time had whirled itself around, and she was suddenly allowed to marry Scott Frampton, just as she'd always planned to back in her teenage years. What more could she want?

"I picked out a few. They're on the rack over there." Amanda pointed a sad finger toward the left-hand side of the boutique.

The woman who owned the boutique made notes to herself near the register. She had hardly grunted a "hello" when Susan had entered. Probably, she was ready to close up for the day, and Amanda had pressed her for more time.

"Okay. I'll try a few on."

Susan wanted nothing less than to stuff herself into a few gowns, especially now that she wanted to sink herself into Marcie Shean's case. She rose up and placed two fingers on either side of the delicate lace of one of the designer gowns. At forty-five, it felt half-ridiculous to put one of these dresses on. They seemed fit for a prom queen.

Susan stepped behind the curtain and removed her burgundy suit. Amanda's feet appeared beneath the curtain as she paced.

"So, where were you, anyway?" Amanda finally asked. "I mean, we didn't have any other appointments on the schedule."

"We had a walk-in, actually."

"Oh?"

Susan pulled off her camisole and blinked at herself in the mirror. Bra, panties, long legs that needed a shave. She hadn't spent the past few nights at Scott's, as she'd needed to look over some documents for the Sunrise Cove with her father and had then fallen into conversation with Lola or Christine or Audrey or Amanda. They had such a cozy club. It made it difficult sometimes for her to return to Scott's quaint cabin by the water.

"Mom? Who was the walk-in?"

Susan sensed already that her daughter would be none-too-pleased about the added workload. Amanda had already cited Susan as the ultimate "workaholic" and had even left a magazine open on her desk, which spoke about the dangers of stress. Her doctor certainly wouldn't be too thrilled. Still, Amanda was one to talk: she loved adding more and more items to her to-do list. It was just the Sheridan-Harris way.

Susan grabbed one of the wedding dresses and shuffled herself into it. Back when she had first married Richard, they'd had only a few pennies to rub together, and she'd worn something she had found on a back rack at a second-hand shop. If she remembered correctly, the dress had cost around seventy-five dollars, and she'd still cursed herself for being so greedy. Life was so different now. She had to be grateful for it.

Susan hardly blinked at herself in the mirror.

"Mom? Are you going to tell me? Or—"

Susan pushed the curtain to the side to reveal herself. She placed her hands on her hips and made heavy eye contact with Amanda, whose face was initially difficult to read. After a long moment of silence, however, Amanda burst into laughter.

"You look like an eighties music video nightmare."

Susan grinned. "Is it that bad?" She stepped out of the little changing area and turned to find a horrible portrait of herself in the mirror. It was true. She looked like a bride from a distant era. The sequins on the garment were totally outdated, and the cut of it was high up on her waist so that she looked much chunkier than her ordinary slim frame.

"I did not put that dress in there!" Amanda howled with laughter and clutched her stomach. "Where did you get that?"

"What? It was hanging in there! Isn't this the one you hung up?"

Tears sprung to Amanda's eyes as she continued to laugh uncontrollably at her mother's appearance. The wedding dress shop owner glared at them. Probably, this dress cost thousands of dollars and was sought-after by some of the ritziest tourists of Martha's Vineyard, hungry for the next era of fashion. Everyone wanted to make a statement. Susan, on the other hand, just needed something white to walk down the aisle in.

"This one is a hard no, Mom," Amanda said finally as she wiped the tears from her cheeks. "How heavy is it?"

Susan shifted up on her toes to feel. "It weighs about as much as a MAC truck, I think."

"I figured. We'd need to tow you down the aisle."

"Are you sure you don't want your mother looking like a nightmare version of Madonna?" Susan asked as she dropped her lower lip out. "Because I think this look could really suit me."

"No!" Amanda cried. Her grin widened. She placed her hands on her hips and heaved a sigh. "Mom, we have to focus. If you're going to get married on June 19, we need to nail all this down. ASAP. Do you understand?"

"Where did that tone come from?" Susan teased. A moment later, she burst out laughing once again and gave her daughter a playful salute.

"If you're going to act like a teenager, then I'm going to treat you like one. I—"

But at that moment, the wedding dress store's door flew open. Christine flourished from the outside world. Her dark hair whirled around her shoulders, and her perfect bohemian style made her look as though she, too, had stepped from a magazine— albeit a much more current and beautiful one. She gripped her knees to catch her breath as Amanda and Susan gaped at her.

"You're late," Amanda chided.

Christine lifted her chin. Tears filled her eyes as she found Susan's gaze. Susan knew something was off, but she had no idea what.

She stepped toward her younger sister and lifted her back to standing. Her brow furrowed when she whispered, "Are you okay, Chris?"

In the corner, the wedding dress shop owner grumbled inwardly. Obviously, she wouldn't make a sale that night, and these women were taking up her much-needed clean-up time.

Finally, Christine pressed her fingers against her eyes as her shoulders quivered. "I'm sorry. I just don't even know how to say it."

Susan drew her head around to find Amanda's gaze. Her heart panged with fear. Already, the Sheridans had been through so much the previous year; Susan herself had only just beaten cancer, and their father, Wes, continued to decline with dementia. What else could possibly happen? What would hit them next?

Christine dropped her hands to her sides. After a long gasp, she said three little words, words upon which the Sheridans could hang endless dreams and hopes.

"I am pregnant."

Chapter Three

The wedding dress shop owner whacked the "CLOSED" sign onto the door just as Susan, Christine, and Amanda hurried out into the growing darkness. Susan flung her arm around Christine and howled to the sky. "You have got to be kidding me, Christine! The odds were stacked against you for so many years! And then suddenly, out of the blue, Zach knocks you up at age forty-two?"

Christine shivered against Susan. "Zach is still in shock. He had to open the bistro tonight, and I swear he keeps messing up. I watched him chop all this garlic and then accidentally throw it into the trash."

Amanda burst into laughter. She jangled her keys from her pocket and beckoned the two of them toward her car. "I don't think either of you can drive right now. You both look giddy."

"Let's let the responsible one take us back home. We can grab our cars tomorrow," Susan said. "I'll text Lola. We need supplies— lots of supplies."

"For what?" Christine asked as she slid into the back seat.

"A celebration! We can't just let this day pass by without doing something about it," Susan affirmed. In a flash, she wrote Lola, who texted back immediately.

> LOLA: A celebration? For what?

> SUSAN: You'll see. It'll blow your socks off.

> LOLA: I'm wearing sandals.

> SUSAN: Omg, just buy wine and snacks. Maybe order a pizza? Hire a mariachi band. We need to celebrate.

> LOLA: You sound insane, sis. Did you buy a dress?

> SUSAN: Just get the stuff.

> LOLA: I hate when you get all big-sister on me.

> SUSAN: Too bad! Just trust me.

Amanda was one of the more responsible drivers Susan had ever known. She remembered even back when she had first taught Amanda how to drive, almost seven years ago or so, when Amanda had kept her hands eternally at ten-and-two and grumbled about anyone else going two or three miles over the speed limit. Susan had laughed at Richard at the time and said, *"Our teenage girl is about to turn into an eighty-five-year-old woman."* *"They grow up so fast,"* Richard had joked in return.

"Do you have the stick with you?" Susan asked from the passenger seat. She yanked around to catch Christine in the midst of another cry.

Christine leafed through her purse for a plastic baggie in which she had placed the pink and white pregnancy test. Sure enough, two bright pink lines declared her uterus baby-ready.

"What did that feel like?" Susan asked, almost breathless.

Christine slipped her teeth over her lower lip. Finally, as Amanda muttered something about an "irresponsible driver up ahead," Christine said, "It felt like all these doors I'd always thought were locked suddenly flew open. Suddenly, I can see a future for myself that I had always hoped for but never truly imagined. And to be fully honest... one of the first things I did was go into my bedroom and look up at the ceiling and started talking to Mom."

Susan's heart swelled at her sister's words. In truth, when she had first gotten pregnant with Jake when she was just a young thing, totally broke with only a boyfriend, and she had the greatest fear of what her future would look like or become— she, too, had spoken to Anna. "Help," had been her general prayer. "I don't know what I'm doing. And I need you here."

"Anyway. It probably sounds crazy," Christine whispered.

"No. It sounds like the most natural thing in the world," Susan assured her.

Back at home, the Sheridan house was dark and shadowed, yet warm from a rather glorious, blue-skied day. The three of them entered the house through the back and found Audrey on the couch with a sleeping Max across her upper chest. His perfect, chubby cheek bulged up from the towel beneath it. Audrey's eyes were tired yet filled with light.

"Hi! Mom should be back soon," she whispered. "She said we're celebrating something?"

Wes's bedroom door was shut downstairs. She pointed at it as Audrey explained that he didn't feel so good. "He coughed a few times this afternoon. I think it's just a cold or something. We're monitoring it."

Audrey rose and headed upstairs to place Max in his crib. She reappeared in a fresh dress with the baby monitor in her right hand. Christine seemed not to know what to do with herself. She hovered near the porch door and drew her hands together. Audrey and Christine— who had a special connection— made heavy eye contact.

"You're acting so weird," Audrey said finally. "Is there something wrong?"

Suddenly, Lola burst through the back door. There was the rustling of plastic bags as she hustled in, armed with bottles of wine and bags of chips in her left hand and two large pizza boxes in her right. She stopped dead in the hallway between the mudroom and the kitchen and blinked at Christine. There was a strange, pregnant silence.

"Oh my God," Lola blurted.

"What?" Christine shifted her weight.

"I know. I know what this is about," Lola breathed. She placed the pizza boxes on the counter. She'd brought with her the growing chill of the evening. Her cheeks were flushed. "You're pregnant, aren't you?"

Audrey screamed as her mother's words registered in her brain. She placed her hands on her cheeks and gave Christine a bug-eyed look. Christine's eyes closed as her shoulders shook. She nodded just once as Audrey flung her arms around Christine's shoulders and held her tight. Lola, Susan, and Amanda hustled over, and together, the five Sheridan girls wrapped themselves into a big, multi-armed ball of love and energy and hope. In no time at all, each of their faces was wet with tears and filled with happiness.

"Music! We need music." Lola rushed toward the side of the room, where she connected her phone to the speaker system. She played one of Christine's favorites—"Angel Baby," but the John Lennon version.

Lola then beckoned for Christine to come out to the center of the living room, where they slow-danced and swayed to the music. Christine tossed her head back so that her long hair swept to the very bottom of her back. Susan touched her hair sheepishly. It had grown out so long since she'd been cleared of cancer, but it still didn't have the luster of her sisters'.

That was what time did to you, Susan thought now. It gave you so many blessings, but it took something for itself, too. In this case: she aged. She grew sick. She championed through. But she hadn't the glow of her twenties. Her eyes were circled with crow's feet. Her back occasionally ached when she slept on it wrong.

The five of them wrapped up in sweaters and blankets and sat around the picnic table on the porch. They took a portable speaker with them and played more "baby-themed" songs, just loud enough to create an ambiance and not loud enough that they woke Wes.

They loaded their plates with all the goods: gooey, cheesy pizza, handfuls of chips, and potato salad. Spring was heavy in the air, and with it came the promise of future BBQs, sizzling bonfires, and nights beneath the splendorous, twinkling night sky. Christine, herself, seemed to glow even brighter than the moon. She placed her hand on her stomach throughout much of the dinner as though she already wanted to keep the little being safe.

"Bad planning, Christine," Audrey teased her. "We should have been pregnant at the same time. It would have been so much more fun. Or at least, not as heinous."

Christine laughed. "I would have been pregnant years ago if I could have. I'm guessing a pregnancy at forty-two won't be the easiest thing in the world."

"Women do it all the time," Lola assured her. "Especially in the bigger cities. Some of my friends in Boston had babies at forty-five and forty-six. The doctor will monitor everything, and we'll keep you safe and cozy."

"And Max will have someone to grow up with!" Audrey said brightly. "They're going to be best friends."

Christine's smile was wider than Susan had ever seen. Back in the early days, Christine had always been the surly Sheridan sister— the darker one, the one apt to drink and stew in the corner. Motherhood would bring out even more of the nuances of her personality. Susan couldn't wait to learn all these new parts about Christine. It would be a journey for all of them.

Lola poured some wine for those who wanted it and a glass of sparkling water for Christine. "I don't know what we'll do without our champion wine-drinker drinking all summer long, but we'll have to make do," Lola teased. "Although I'm sure the wine industry will really suffer."

"Stop..." Christine laughed outright as she lifted her sparkling water. "I'm sure the wine industry will survive without me."

"But in all seriousness, I want to make a toast to my older sister." Lola beamed. "Nobody in the world deserves this happiness more than you. We will be by your side every single day that ticks by. And Baby Sheridan-Walters? We love you to pieces."

Something weighed heavily on Susan's mind. After the toast, she sipped her wine and then headed inside for a moment, where she traced a path toward the upstairs trunk. There, she discovered their mother, Anna's diaries, which were dated all the way back to before Susan was born. She muttered to herself as she hunted for the one she had in mind. In a moment, she found it: dark gray leather on the outside, worn from everyday opening and closing. Even the pages were yellowed and weathered with wrinkles.

Back downstairs, Susan placed the diary on the table and collapsed back in her chair.

"What do you have there?" Lola asked as she lifted her glass of wine.

"Mom's diary?" Christine furrowed her brow.

"Yes. From the year she was pregnant with you," Susan clarified.

"Susan Sheridan! You're too much." Christine reached for the diary and flipped through the pages as tears welled in her eyes. "I just told Amanda and Susan that one of the first things I did was talk to Mom when I found out."

Lola nodded. "I did the same." She reached over and squeezed Audrey's hand over the table. "Gosh, it's just one of the saddest things in the world that our mother can't know the both of you. And baby Max. And Baby Walters-Sheridan."

Christine cleared her throat. The others grew silent and turned toward her.

"She wrote this when she was about seven months

pregnant with me, it looks like," Christine breathed. "She says, 'It's so very late, but Susan is up with a horrible ear infection and Wes has to man the front desk tonight. Here I am in this big house, alone with a pregnant belly and a toddler. Sometimes, the loneliness of being the person who has to be strong, the strongest of all, gets to be too much— but then I look in Susan's eyes and I know it's all worth it. What Wes and I have built here is a tremendous amount of love, probably more love than I deserve.

I try to imagine what this baby will be like. We've decided again not to learn the sex. Wes is fully on board for a boy, but I have already begun to imagine two little girls in matching dresses, holding hands as we walk along the water. There's such a beauty— and a horror of being a woman. We must be strong yet feminine. We must bear life and thus bear an infinite amount of sadness. I worry already about the tremendous amounts of pain my girls will go through. I worry about the heartaches and the fears. I worry so endlessly— which is almost a relief because it means that I no longer worry so much about myself. Maybe that's the secret of motherhood. At least, for a little while, you no longer look in the mirror. You see only the ones who need you.'"

Christine lifted her eyes to the other women at the table. Not a single eye remained dry.

"She was such a poet, wasn't she?" Christine breathed.

The five of them held hands after that. They closed their eyes and prayed, each of them quietly, their heads filled with sorrow, longing, joy, and fear. In a way, Anna Sheridan sat along with them. In a way, she had been there with them all along.

Chapter Four

Amanda hovered over Susan's desk with her hands on her hips as Susan explained the events that had transpired the previous afternoon, prior to her departure from the office. Susan had printed countless documents about the case, which were currently spread across her desk, including information about the selected jury members, along with testimonials about the lawyer the boy's family had hired for the case. It was essential that Susan understand the working mind of this lawyer so that she could potentially perceive how he might act in a court of law and what mechanisms he might use to convince the jury that Marcie Shean had committed this heinous act. She had also contacted Marcie's previous lawyer; his office had assured her that they would courier over the files the following day.

Even now, she caught Amanda's eyes glittering with excitement. "This is big, Mom."

Susan leaned back in her chair, then looked up at her daughter with a grin. "I know."

Amanda paced for a moment, back and forth in front

of the desk. "I mean, it's big in about a million different ways. It's a huge, high-profile case, and it would definitely sky-rocket your name into the legal stratosphere, you know?"

"Oh, I know." Susan had worked high-profile cases before, but mostly, she'd worked alongside Richard, and both of them had received accolades. This would be mostly just her. It thrilled her.

"But beyond that, it's going to take up so much of your time. Have you looked into why Marcie lost her lawyer in the first place? What happened there?"

In truth, Susan didn't really care why Marcie's previous lawyer had dropped her case. It sounded like it was a personal issue. She only worried about the files arriving safely and in time. She shivered but set her jaw and said, "I haven't been allowed to sink my teeth into a challenge like this in years."

"But you're not just doing it for the thrill of it, right? Because there are other things you could get thrills out of, you know. Like picking out a wedding dress? Or letting Christine know what you want for your wedding cake? At least the flavor or icing."

Susan rolled her eyes all the way back as Amanda giggled.

"I know. Silly of me to ask. This is clearly where your heart is," Amanda said. She then began to gather up the papers as she muttered, "But you won't be able to do it without me. This—" Amanda's hand circled over her mother's desk, which was strewn with papers everywhere, "is so unorganized, Mom. I don't know how you managed before without me."

"I guess Penelope had something to do with all that

organization," Susan admitted as she squinted her eyes playfully.

"Mom!"

Penelope was, of course, the secretary Richard had left Susan for. She was now thirty-two years old and pregnant with their first child. The news of this had reached them around the time of Amanda's failed wedding, which meant that Penelope was about half as big as a whale.

Still, it had been a long time since Susan had felt any resentment toward either of them. They had gone for the cliché: husband falls for secretary, leaves longtime wife scenario. But Susan had gone for her own cliché. She'd decided instead to create a new life for herself and find real happiness with a man who would love her unconditionally for the rest of her days. They'd all gotten exactly what they had wanted.

Except for Richard, maybe. He had already raised two kids! Susan had thanked her lucky stars above when the days of sticky car seats and all-day soccer matches had ended.

"So, I'll have these organized for you; I'll make copies, and I'll call up the previous lawyer if our files don't arrive tomorrow?" Amanda said from the door.

Susan nodded. "Sounds great."

"Are you coming home for dinner?"

"No. I have to see Scott tonight! We keep missing each other," Susan said. Her heart ballooned with excitement. How she longed to hold Scott in her arms and speak to him about this upcoming court case and Christine's new baby, and how everything she'd ever dreamed of seemed to be happening for her right now.

* * *

A Vineyard Wedding

Susan texted Scott when she left the office.

> SUSAN: I'm headed to you! See you soon.

But when she glanced at her phone a few seconds later, she realized that the message had only one "checkmark," which meant that the message hadn't gone to Scott's phone. She had never seen the likes of this before. Always, Scott was a responsible guy, the kind who brought a backup charger and never left the house unless his phone battery was at eighty percent or higher.

Susan drove over to Scott's little cabin as the radio sizzled through various old tracks from the eighties. When she pulled into Scott's driveway, she found it lifeless, and the cabin itself was empty. Her stomach felt hollow and strange. When she walked up to the front door, she found it locked. Normally, Scott didn't even bother locking it. She lifted her keys from her pocket and weaved her way inside, where she found a house in a state of mid-morning chaos. A half-eaten bowl of oatmeal sat on the table; the bed remained unmade. A bath towel was stretched across the ground as though Scott had flung it off himself on the hunt for pants.

Susan texted him again.

> SUSAN: Hey. Are you okay?

She still only saw one checkmark. Susan shivered and walked to the counter, where she opened a bottle of wine. As Scott didn't have any wine glasses, she poured the wine into a coffee mug and stared out across the waves. It wasn't a particularly beautiful day; clouds were heavy on the horizon, and the waves rolled toward the sands ominously, as though designed to hurt.

Was it possible that Scott had been injured? Susan swallowed the lump in her throat, along with her wine, and tried to think about what to do next. Perhaps she could call the hospital? She reached for her phone and dialed Christine, who she knew had decided to help Zach that night at the bistro.

"Hey, Chris."

On the other line, there was the hustle and bustle, the endless laughter and chatter, of the bistro as the evening shift flourished.

"Hey, girl! What's up?" She sounded breathless.

"I was wondering if you'd seen Scott around the Inn at all?"

"Gosh, no. I walked right into the bistro and Zach put me to work."

"All right. Tell him not to work you too hard. You're carrying his baby, after all."

Christine laughed, then spoke to someone else, saying, "Yes, we have your four-top ready. You'll have to speak to Ronny up at the front of the house." She then returned to the phone and added, "Is anything wrong? You can't find Scott?"

Susan feigned a laugh. "It's no problem. I'm sure he's around here somewhere. I'm just trying to track my fiancé down because I'm hungry for dinner."

"Well, let me know when you find him. I gotta run. Love you."

"Love you, too."

Susan sipped her wine and continued to gaze out the window at the driveway as though it could produce Scott at any moment. Her heart pounded heavier. In a moment, she called both Amanda and Audrey, neither of whom had seen nor heard from Scott. In the background, Max wept, and Audrey hurried off to take care of him. Susan felt so alone after she hung up.

But just as she gathered her things to head out to her car and trace her path back home, she spotted Scott's truck at the far end of the driveway. She stopped on the porch and watched, unable to lift the sides of her lips for any kind of smile. Midway down the driveway, she realized there was a second person in the truck. She tilted her head until it came fully into view. And in a moment, after the engine stopped and Scott unlocked the doors, none other than Scott's teenage son, Kellan, stepped out of the truck. Susan hadn't seen him in quite some time— maybe not since Christmas, as Kellan lived with his mother up in Boston and was busy with school.

Kellan looked different. His hair was longer and unkept; his legs and arms seemed longer and lankier; and his shoulders sagged, as though the weight of the world was too much for him. He lifted his chin so that his eyes connected with Susan's, but he didn't return her smile.

It was clear that something had gone very wrong.

Scott hustled up the front walkway and then up the stairs. Out of breath, he said, "Susan, I'm so sorry. I left my stupid phone at the Inn, and I just only realized it when I was on the road to Boston."

"Don't worry about it," Susan assured him, even as her throat tightened. "I see we have a visitor?"

Scott turned back as Kellan mounted the steps.

"What do you think, champ? You want to order some food?" She could see Scott was trying to step back into his role as Dad but slightly failing by the look on Kellan's face.

"I'll grab some of the menus," Susan said. "Mexican? Chinese? Thai? Pick your poison."

Scott gave her a wonderful smile, even as her insides threatened to pop. He squeezed her upper arm as he led Kellan into the house. Once inside, Susan found the food menus in a little basket and splayed them out for Kellan, who seemed to not care at all what was for dinner.

"I'll go grab your backpack," Scott said. "While you decide."

Susan followed Scott out toward the truck. All the way, Scott was dead silent. She could feel the turbulence of his head as it swirled wildly. Once at the truck, he drew the top up and blinked into the darkness.

"Scott." Susan stood beside him but felt they were separated by oceans. "Scott, are you going to talk to me?"

Scott closed his eyes. "It's been a hell of a day."

Susan splayed her hand across his back. At her touch, he actually flinched— something he had never done. She felt strangely uncomfortable and unwelcomed at that moment.

"I started hearing about this only last week. I haven't been able to fully comprehend it," Scott began. "But apparently, Kellan has had some serious trouble at school."

Susan's eyes widened. "What kind of trouble?"

"Well, I guess he was bullied a lot." Scott scrunched his nose. The pain of it seemed extraordinary. "And recently, he's started to fight back— rather violently."

Susan's heart dropped. Although she didn't know Kellan well, he had always been such a kind, pleasant, artistic kid. The previous summer, she had watched as he and her father, Wes, had swapped stories about the birds they liked the best, as both frequently bird-watched.

"I guess he just snapped," Scott said. "I can't say I fully blame him. They put him through a lot. But apparently, if he didn't move school districts, his mother was going to agree to have him put in a juvenile detention facility."

"What?" Susan was totally taken aback. "Juvie?"

Scott nodded. "She told me this afternoon. I totally lost my mind, so I got in my truck and headed straight to Boston. We had his bag packed in five minutes. My ex howled at me the whole time. She said there was no way she could handle him anymore. Said that I never should have stayed on 'this stupid island,' and I should have followed her to Boston like a real man to take care of our son. In a way, I feel she's right. But I need to be there for him, now."

Susan's mouth went completely dry. Scott smacked the top of the truck back down and gathered Kellan's backpack across his back. "We'll have to go back to Boston to get the rest of his stuff. It was just so rushed. And I didn't want it to feel like whiplash to him, you know? That's the only home he's known for years, and he barely remembers the island, other than the short visit last year."

Susan felt herself nod as Scott stepped back toward the house. He glanced around as though he waited for her to come up. But she just waved a hand.

"It seems like you two have a lot to talk about," she said. "I don't want to get in the way. He probably thinks I'll never understand any of it."

Scott dropped his shoulders. His eyes searched hers. She wanted to tell him that she would understand when the time was right, but right now, he needed time alone with Kellan to work things out between them. She could feel the emotions in the air, and she didn't want to add any stress to his already chaotic day.

But now that Kellan was fully in Scott's life without him even asking her about it beforehand— what did that mean for Susan? According to Amanda (the ever-responsible note-taker and calendar-maker), Susan and Scott's wedding was only six weeks away. But this felt like another nail in some kind of coffin. Susan's heart felt heavy with doom.

Chapter Five

Susan latched the door closed at the Sheridan house and listened for the familiar creaks as it allowed the ocean breeze to mold and shift the floors and walls. The house seemed empty. No laughter billowed out from the back porch, the television wasn't on, and nothing brewed on the stovetop. Thusly, when Susan stepped into the living area and discovered Lola, with her long naked legs stretched out in front of her on the floor, her back against the bottom of the sofa, and baby Max in the crook of her arm, she was initially startled yet grateful to see them there. She was grateful that someone was home and awake.

"Hi!" Lola had removed her makeup and looked somehow more youthful. She blinked large eyes up at Susan and nodded toward baby Max. "He's been out for twenty minutes, but I've been too afraid to move. Didn't think you were coming home, though? Amanda said you were headed to Scott's."

"Yeah, I was." Susan buzzed her lips and reached for

some sparkling water on the counter. She poured them two glasses, then sat on the floor across from Lola, who assessed her with a furrowed brow.

"Something's wrong."

Susan shrugged. "I don't know. No. It doesn't really matter."

Lola sipped her water as the silence stretched between them. "You know, we've been through too much to keep secrets from each other."

"True." Susan rolled a bit of the liquid across her tongue as she considered this. "Scott's son is here. It seems like he might be here for a while, and I'm not sure what to think about it."

"Phew." Lola's eyebrows shot toward her hairline. "A teenage boy in your life."

"Yep."

"That's a doozy for sure."

"I don't know how to process it. So I might just throw myself totally into work."

"Amanda is going to kill you if you don't finalize stuff for the wedding."

"Maybe there won't even be—"

"Hey. Don't talk like that." Lola shook her head delicately. Again, they shared a moment of silence. "Why don't you tell me about this case? Amanda said there's a new, big one—"

"Boston. Twenty-five-year-old girl who supposedly murdered her boyfriend."

Lola's lips formed an O. "You're telling me your client is Marcie Shean?"

"You know about this?"

"This has been the hottest topic in Boston since

November," Lola affirmed. "Everyone has their own opinion about it, but most people tend to think, well..."

"What?"

"That she did it."

Susan chuckled. "Great."

"Just saying. You're up against a whole city of opinions," Lola said. "So the girl is here? On the island?"

"Yeah. She's currently on house arrest. I'm supposed to meet her tomorrow."

Lola was impressed. Susan still kind of liked that feeling of impressing her younger sisters. She supposed it never really disappeared.

"She's a beautiful girl," Lola said as Max whimpered in her arms. "I guess that's either in your favor or a detriment. She's either too beautiful and, therefore, the obvious villain, or she's so beautiful that she can't be anything but innocent. In the eyes of the jury, that is."

"So you're saying it could go either way? Gee, thanks." Susan grinned wider, grateful to speak about something that wasn't her fiancé's troubled teenager.

"You know, one of my friends up in Boston covers that case for the paper," Lola said. "You should talk to her. She knows just about everything there is to know about the case, and I'm sure you feel rushed as it is. Maybe she could fill in the gaps."

"That would be fantastic," Susan said. "Really."

"Bet you never thought your baby sister would swing in for the assist?"

"I never thought I'd see my baby sister become a grandmother," Susan retorted. "But look at you. You're a natural."

"Just have to dye my hair blue and get a perm, like the

other grannies," Lola, who looked fit for any fashion magazine, joked.

"Are you staying here tonight? Or is Tommy expecting you?" Susan lifted up from the ground to grab a snack from the counter— homemade granola bars, which were Amanda's newfound specialty.

"He expects me. The girls should be back from their dates—"

"Dates?" Susan's heart jumped.

"I mean, they'd never call them dates. But they're hanging out with Sam and that other guy from the NICU. Noah."

Susan arched an eyebrow. "Leave it to Audrey to meet some handsome man at the NICU, huh?"

Lola grinned. "The apple doesn't fall so far from the tree, I guess. I can't really pick her apart for it, and besides, she's only twenty. I like seeing her out and about. I like seeing her happy. It's been such a hard year for all of us. One day at a time, right?"

* * *

The following morning, just after nine, Susan watched herself in horror as she accidentally spilled a huge drop of piping-hot coffee across her blouse. She remained in her car, stationed just outside of the house in which Marcie Shean lived out her house arrest until her trial began.

"Shoot. Shoot!" Susan scrambled for an answer to her growing stain. A tissue? A white-out cleaning pen? But her purse revealed no assistance. The brown stain was a clear testament to her nerves.

Susan gripped her suit jacket and yanked it tighter across her chest so that it covered up about half of the stain. She then headed out of her car and traced the path up toward the porch. Perhaps, due to the stain, she should have asked to reschedule. First impressions were everything. But she also knew that Marcie didn't have much of an option. It was either Susan-the-Stain or nobody.

Just before Susan could ring the bell, Mr. Shean himself pulled open the door. He stood, a domineering force in the doorway, wearing an old Boston University sweatshirt with a large stain of its own near the armpit.

"Morning," he greeted with a half-smile. "Thanks for coming by." His tone didn't feel sincere at all.

Susan stepped into the foyer. Already from there, she sensed that this wasn't exactly a happy house. It seemed overly shadowed with the curtains drawn over most of the windows. The walls had some cracks in the plaster, with only a single photo hanging on the wall, presumably of the mother who had long ago passed away. There was also a dank, moldy smell that permeated through the air. Susan did her best to maintain her professional air.

A teenage boy snaked past her. He wore sweatpants and no shirt, and the dim light from the television made him look a little creepy.

"Turn that off," his father growled. "We have company."

The boy just fell back on the couch and did no such thing. He didn't even lift his eyes.

"Marcie is in her bedroom," Mr. Shean said. "Upstairs. I'll lead you."

Susan followed Mr. Shean up the steps and onto the landing. A door was hung with bright pink beads, presumably from a bright teenage past. Mr. Shean knocked on the door and hollered, "Your lawyer is here." Horrible words to hear, Susan knew.

The girl who opened the door didn't look much like the girl in the newspaper. She wore no makeup, her cheeks were gaunt and tight, and her eyes were large and sad, like a trapped animal's. She wore a light pink zip-up sweatshirt and a pair of leggings, along with socks that didn't match. She just looked like an innocent girl, albeit a scared one, certainly not a murderer.

But of course, nobody really looked like the crimes they'd committed. Susan knew that from her many years in the field.

"Hi Marcie," Susan said. She lifted her portfolio in greeting. "It's good to meet you."

Marcie gave no smile, but she did step back and gesture for Susan to enter. Susan did and with her steps inward, she found herself inside a similar teenage fantasy. Old movie posters and magazine cut-outs adorned the far wall, ones from maybe seven or eight years ago. Susan knew them because Amanda herself had been into them, although she was a tiny bit younger than this girl. It was like stepping through time.

Marcie sat on the bed. "You can sit here if you like." She pointed at the desk chair across from her, which had a massive sticker across the back that read: I HEART VEGAN.

A vegan murderer? It was possible.

Susan sat and spread her portfolio out across her lap. When she looked up, she found Marcie's large green eyes, zeroing in on the stain on her shirt. Susan had somehow forgotten it en route from the car. She tapped the still-wet brown spot and said, "I got a little clumsy this morning."

Marcie nodded but didn't smile.

"Anyway, I was hoping I could ask you a few questions today, so I can get a better handle on the case as a whole," Susan explained. "But before we get started, do you have any questions for me? I know it's important for us to trust one another."

Marcie stuck her tongue into the inside of her right cheek so that it bulged out. After a pause, Marcie shook her head. "I don't think so," she added.

"I mean, you can ask about my past history?" Susan began.

Marcie shrugged.

"I've worked as a criminal defense lawyer for the previous twenty years," Susan said, deciding to give at least a little bit of background. She hoped it would put the girl at ease a little more, even if she didn't think she needed to hear it. "I've had hundreds of clients and I've enjoyed the work immensely."

"Cool." That was all she replied.

This wasn't exactly what Susan had wanted to hear. Still, there was no way to sense what a young girl like this thought in such a situation. Depression was probably too small of a term.

Susan clicked the top of her pen absently. There was a hardness to this girl that maybe others wouldn't have seen. She had built thick walls around herself. How would Susan dig into them? How would she work with this girl?

"I want you to know that I will do everything in my power to prove your innocence," Susan said finally.

The girl just blinked at her. Susan placed her pen on her pad of paper and said, "Okay. I am sure this has happened to you numerous times already. But I really need to hear everything in your words, here and now. What happened on the afternoon of November 13?"

"I came back to the apartment, and he was dead."

Susan drew her eyes back toward Marcie's. They seemed hollow, as though she'd already cried out all the tears she possibly could.

"And now I'm on trial for his murder," she added.

Susan tried another approach. "Was there anyone that your boyfriend was talking about? Anyone who might have had something to do with this? Anyone who frightened your boyfriend, any enemies?"

This time, Marcie just shrugged. "He had a lot of friends. Some people didn't like him. I don't know. He was just a regular guy, in a way. A complete idiot other times, for sure."

"Idiot. Why do you say that?"

"I'm sure you've read that Vincent and I didn't exactly see eye-to-eye toward the end."

"All couples fight, don't they?" Susan said.

"Sure. But most couples get out of it alive," Marcie replied.

Susan furrowed her brow. Was this some kind of admission? Did Marcie want to insinuate that, actually, she'd been the one to stab Vincent?

"Where were you before you found him?"

"At the store."

"And what did you do after you found him?"

For the first time, Marcie's eyes brimmed with tears. "I wrapped myself around him and took out the knife and —well." She shook her head. "I don't know. I think I blacked out for a while. I must have called someone because the cops were there shortly afterward. Everything after that is kind of a blur. Like I drank too much or something."

At that moment, the girl's chin dropped toward her chest as a sob escaped. Susan felt a wave of pity for this poor creature. She wasn't entirely sure where she was in terms of believing her story or not. One thing she did believe, though, was that Marcie didn't deserve a life in prison.

Well, she had to believe that. It was her job to believe that beyond a shadow of a doubt.

Chapter Six

Susan created a large bulletin board of information she had drawn up for Marcie Shean's case. Thankfully, Marcie's previous lawyer had sent over all of his research— which, admittedly, wasn't very much— and she'd also read about a zillion newspaper articles, read about all jury members, and even interviewed a few people who'd grown up with Marcie on the island. Naturally, there was still a lot to do, but Susan now felt more on top of the case than ever.

She now stood in front of the bulletin board as her heart hammered in her chest. At the center of the large space, she had placed that world-famous photograph of Marcie; those big, frightened green eyes peered out at the world, and her beauty told a sinister story. What had really happened that fateful day? Susan wasn't sure she would ever truly know.

There was a rap at the door. Susan had fallen so deep into her thoughts that the sound made her yelp. She hustled toward it and pulled it open to find Amanda, who gave her a silly smile.

"I haven't heard from you in a while. You okay in here?"

A blush crept up Susan's neck and dipped onto her cheeks. "I think I got a bit lost in the case again."

Amanda laughed good-naturedly. "I figured as much. You want to talk anything out?"

Susan gestured toward the board. "Well, to be honest, I really need to get myself up to Boston. I want to interview the people the couple knew. Get a better sense of them before the murder happened. The version of Marcie Shean that people know around here isn't necessarily the version she was up in Boston. But people change."

"True," Amanda said thoughtfully. She stepped toward the board and straightened out a crinkled edge of the photograph of Marcie. "She's really beautiful."

"I can't imagine her getting life in prison," Susan murmured as her heart swelled. "You should have seen her in her childhood bedroom. The house was a mess. It's obvious she ran away from the Vineyard for a reason. And now, she's trapped on house arrest."

"Such a horrible story," Amanda murmured.

Susan stepped toward her desk again and reached for a pen to jot herself a note.

"So, are we still on for later?" Amanda asked then.

Susan furrowed her brow as she lifted her head from her pad of paper. "I'm sorry?"

"Mom, come on. We have to get you a wedding dress sometime."

"Oh. That's right. I think it will work." Susan glanced again at her calendar, which seemed to fill up more and more as the days passed.

"We're leaving here at five sharp. That's final!" Amanda said then as she stepped back toward the foyer.

"I'm serious, Mom. Someone has to take charge of your wedding and if it's not you, then I guess that someone has to be me."

"You're wise beyond your years, Amanda Harris," Susan breathed.

But a minute later, Susan's phone blared. It was Scott. She hadn't seen him since the previous afternoon when he had stopped by to have lunch at her office. He had spoken exclusively about his son— without a single mention of the wedding. It was obvious that he was worried. Kellan was meant to begin school at Oak Bluffs High that day. "He was bullied so much back in Boston. I just hope the kids here take some kind of liking to him. I don't know. It was always so easy for me, you know? I had so many friends. I had you. But Kellan has nobody, and he seems to want to live life like an island— alone."

Susan hadn't really known what to say. Her thoughts were a whirlwind. She wanted to be there for Scott in every way, but she really hadn't accounted for this possibility. A teenage boy! In her life!

"Hey!" Susan said brightly as she answered the phone. "What's up?"

Scott held the silence for a moment before he answered. "Susan. I hate to ask this of you. I really do."

Susan's heart sank. Out the window, a bird landed on the nearest branch and seemed to stare directly through the glass and into her eyes, mocking her.

"What's wrong, Scott?"

"It's just that, well. You know Kellan started school today?"

"Yes."

"Well. He seems to have— erm— already gotten into a

bit of trouble. The principal just called. He needs to be picked up."

Susan wanted to scream. She maintained eye contact with that bird and tried to tell herself to keep her tone light. It wouldn't do anyone any good for her to lose her cool.

"I see. Do you know what happened?"

"I don't. Not really. But the thing is, I'm in Falmouth right now, gathering supplies. I won't be back on the island for another four hours because we have to wait for this shipment. I wondered if you could, well. Only if it isn't too much trouble—"

"I'll go pick him up. Sure." Susan's nostrils flared. "Should you call the principal and let him know ahead of time?"

"I already told him you were coming," Scott replied.

How presumptuous, Susan thought. This wasn't like Scott. Normally, he was incredibly respectful of her time and her allegiance to her work. Still, it was true. She had time to head over to the high school, pick up this delinquent, and bring him back to the Sheridan house.

"Okay. Sure."

"Susan?"

"Yeah?"

"Thank you. Seriously, I'm kind of in over my head right now. It's like I blinked, and Kellan turned into a raging teenager who gets into trouble at every corner."

Susan wasn't sure how to respond. There was nothing appropriate to say. Teenagers sometimes flipped like switches. Sometimes, young women murdered their boyfriends in cold blood. Other times, people cheated on spouses they loved with everything in them. People did strange things. And she supposed that people like her and Amanda were left to pick up the pieces.

When Susan explained the situation to Amanda in the foyer, Amanda glowered. "First of all, this is crazy. You aren't this kid's mom, and you've met him twice."

"Yes, but I'll be his stepmother soon. Supposedly."

Amanda huffed. "Second of all, you're supposed to go with me to pick out a wedding dress!"

"I know. But I promise that we'll find time next week, sweetie. Trust me. I'm trying my best."

Amanda held Susan's gaze for a long time. It felt like a funny role reversal, as though Amanda wanted to shame her mother into doing her bidding as a mother might. But Susan drew her purse over her shoulder and then headed toward the door, hollering, "I'll see you at dinner?"

Susan drove her car around the roundabout located nearest the front entrance to the high school. She clearly remembered her mother drawing her car to precisely this place for pick-up, back when Susan had gotten hit by a rogue baseball during gym class and had gone home with a horrible headache. She had hardly been able to walk to the vehicle. She had been maybe fifteen at the time. Anna had been two years from the end of her life. Nobody had known any different.

Kellan appeared on the sidewalk. He walked with his shoulders hunched and his cheeks sucked in. The principal, a man Susan had gone to high school with called Jefferson Ritter, marched alongside him, and his belly protruded the slightest bit from his belt. When they reached Susan's car, Kellan slid into the back as Susan pressed the button to open the passenger window. The principal leaned down to speak.

"Hey there, Susan. It's been a while," Jefferson Ritter said.

Susan had only ever half-liked Jefferson. His eyes had roamed strangely when they'd been teenagers. She'd always had the sense that he had wicked things on his mind.

"Hey, Jeff. Thanks for bringing him out."

"Not a problem. I know it's difficult sometimes for a young person to start at a new school," Jefferson continued. He then hollered back, "But we're going to get used to each other, aren't we, Kellan?"

Kellan gave no answer. The silence felt hollow. Susan tried on her brightest, most fake smile and waved a hand. "See you around, Jefferson."

"Hopefully not too soon!" Jefferson said as he chuckled. "Take care."

Susan weaved her car back toward the main road without a word. In the back seat, Kellan leaned so far back so that his long legs shot out in front of him like a spider's.

"Aren't we going back to my dad's?" Kellan finally asked as he noticed the route had shifted a bit.

"No. We're going to my house," Susan told him pointedly. "I don't want to hang out at your dad's house until he gets home."

"I just need some stuff there."

"Like what?" Susan wasn't particularly up for playing games with this kid.

"Like my guitar."

"I think you'll be okay without it for the afternoon."

In response, Kellan mimicked her by putting on a soft, lilting voice as he said, "I think you'll be okay without it for the afternoon."

Susan glared at his eyes in the rearview. "I wish you

luck if you put on that attitude back at my place. My dad might be an old man now, but he used to have a wicked temper."

Kellan didn't respond.

Susan parked outside the Sheridan house and walked inside without waiting for Kellan. She swirled with a strange mix of anger and confusion. She craved dropping back into the case again. At least there, she thought very little about Scott and their future together, with or without Kellan. She thought little about the sudden communication breakdown between them. She felt like she was in limbo.

"Who's there?" Wes's voice came out from the living room as Susan entered.

"Hi, Dad." Susan dropped down and kissed her father on the cheek. He looked so pleasant and kind with those soft eyes. He wore a beautiful, knitted sweater— one that Anna had assuredly made for him— and watched an old baseball game on the TV. Beside him, Audrey was curled up beneath a blanket, fast asleep. Her eyes danced beneath her eyelids.

"We're having a lazy day," Wes told her.

"Looks so cozy," Susan replied.

"Sure is. Audrey made cookies. Help yourself."

"Wow. Audrey, baking?"

"She says she'll be a good mother, the kind who bakes and makes crafts," Wes said with a funny smile. "I told her Baby Max won't want to make a stupid clay pot for a few more years, but she said she wants to get ahead of it."

Kellan appeared in the living room. There was a dark cloud surrounding him, and his eyes pointed toward Wes angrily. Wes's eyebrows drew high in surprise.

"I didn't know we had a visitor. Hi there, Kellan."

Again, Susan was surprised that her father remembered the boy's name. They'd met a few times, but Wes's dementia had only gotten worse since the previous meeting. Probably, Audrey's memory exercises with Wes did him good.

Kellan didn't respond. He sauntered toward the cookie jar and took two. He then gazed out the window, his eyes glazed with boredom.

Susan made eye contact with her father and shrugged. She then mouthed, "I'll explain later," as Wes shrugged and returned his attention to the baseball game. Susan was reminded of having a previous version of Christine around— the teenage Christine, who'd wanted to make everyone else just as unhappy as she was. The difference, of course, was that Susan loved Christine unequivocally. She wasn't even sure she liked Kellan right then.

"Kellan, do you want something to read?" Susan asked. "We have plenty of books on the shelf."

Kellan didn't answer. This apparent habit of his, to ignore questions, poured gasoline over Susan's already-present anger.

"Cool. Well, just don't get in anyone's way, I guess." Her voice was heavy with snark.

Around five-thirty, Lola and Christine both arrived at the house. Both had been pre-warned about the Kellan Situation, and Christine had armed herself with pizza, bags of chips, and a two-liter of soda. A few minutes later, both Zach and Tommy arrived, and they decided to set up another table outside on the back porch to allow for the large family to gather. Just as the pizza boxes were opened, Amanda entered the house. Again, she grumbled to Susan that she couldn't believe they had missed another wedding dress appointment. She then turned a sharp gaze toward Kellan, who sat swiping his thumb across his phone screen in a bored manner.

"If only he knew." Amanda clucked.

"Shh. Don't worry about it," Susan returned.

Audrey bucked up from the couch a few minutes later. She rubbed her eyes, then fled up the stairs to check on Max, who'd apparently slept right along with her. Ten minutes later, she had him propped up against her as she eased through the growing crowd of Sheridan family members. Max buzzed his lips playfully and blinked those big, beautiful blue eyes. Kellan glanced up at him and then turned his eyes toward Audrey.

"How old are you?" he demanded of Audrey, insinuating she was too young to be a mom.

Audrey wasn't exactly the kind of person you messed with. She could take it and give it.

"Twenty. And I'm guessing by the acne on your chin that you're around fifteen?"

Kellan's face flushed crimson, then almost turned to stone at her retort. He returned his gaze to his phone and muttered words nobody could hear. Audrey caught Susan's eye and said, "Who's the teenage dirtbag?"

"Come on, everyone. Let's go outside," Susan said. There was brewing chaos, and the eye of the storm seemed to be Kellan Frampton. She was suddenly reminded of Chuck, Scott's brother, who now served many years in prison for stealing from many island residents, including the Sunrise Cove.

Kellan arrived at the table last. He grunted as he slipped into the last seat, there between Tommy and Amanda. Amanda glowered as he sat. She took a small bite of pizza and looked on the verge of saying exactly what was on her mind. Others at the table, however, sprung into easy conversation. Lola talked about the article she was now in the midst of writing, which discussed the new Hesson House, a mansion-turned-boutique hotel slated to open on the coast over by Edgartown in July.

"You should see the way Olivia Hesson is transforming that place," Lola said. "You can feel the history of the architecture in every room, but it also has this really unique, modern flair. I fell in love with it."

Zach and Christine were bubbling with excitement with everything they discussed. It would be a huge year for them, as they planned to take over care of Baby Max in the fall and then welcome a baby of their own.

"Zach needs a whole lot more practice on the diaper thing," Audrey said as Max cooed in his little baby carrier near the door. "Last time, I swear you asked where the duct tape was to secure it."

Zach rolled his eyes. "That is a gross exaggeration. Yes, I needed to do a re-do that time, but I think there was a design flaw on that particular diaper."

"Oh, sure. Just like a man to blame his failure on someone else," Audrey teased.

Kellan groaned and leaned back, dropping his slice of pizza back on the plate. All eyes turned toward him, the stranger at the table.

"Is something wrong?" Susan finally asked.

Kellan rolled his eyes. "I just don't know why we have to talk about this stupid baby stuff. And also, this pizza is disgusting. Is this really the best the island can do? Because it's even worse than what we had the other night."

Christine's jaw dropped. Lola placed her napkin over

her mouth, seemingly to hide her laughter. Susan's rage returned in a flash.

But it was Wes who spoke first.

"Excuse me, young man, but I'm going to have to ask you to leave the table if you're going to be this rude and disrespectful."

All eyes turned to Wes. He glared at Kellan with an infinite amount of stoicism. Kellan furrowed his brow and jumped up from the table as Wes added, "You will not talk to anyone in this house with such lack of respect again. Do you understand me?"

Kellan grumbled and stepped toward the door. Once inside the house, he slammed it shut, then stomped up the stairs. A few minutes after, there was the sound of a stereo, probably the one in Christine's old bedroom. Nirvana was cranked too loud.

"Well, at least he appreciates my old music collection," Christine said with an awkward smile.

"Idiot," Amanda murmured.

"He's just a kid," Zach affirmed.

"Yes, but he's not our kid," Lola said.

"He will be soon enough." Susan heaved a sigh and turned her eyes out toward the water. She had no idea what to do about this. The kid had nowhere else to go, but he was certainly a thorn in her backside.

Chapter Seven

Scott arrived to pick Kellan up just after eight. Susan stood off to the side of the driveway with her arms crossed over her chest as Kellan leaped into Scott's truck. Scott looked at Susan with guilt marring his face. He knew he'd messed up.

"I'm so sorry about today, Susan," he said. He reached for her elbow and held it tenderly. "I really wish I could have been there."

Susan gave a half-hearted shrug. "He seems really unhappy here."

"He seems just really unhappy everywhere," Scott returned sadly. "I don't know what to do. He won't talk to me."

"Do you think therapy is an option?"

"He is resistant to the idea. And his mom hates when I bring it up," Scott said. "But I think it's one of the only ways forward."

Susan allowed silence to brew between them.

"I just hope you know that I love you. And I want everything to go the way we planned," Scott said.

"I love you, too."

Scott pressed a kiss onto her lips. He then jumped back toward his truck and eased it back down the driveway. Susan lifted a hand to wave goodbye, but neither Scott nor Kellan noticed. She shuddered with fear. She hated that she was suddenly reminded of the anxiety she had felt when she'd learned Richard was cheating on her with Penelope, the secretary. How foolish she'd felt.

Back inside, Lola appeared from the kitchen and handed her a glass of wine. Susan dropped her shoulders forward. "I guess you could tell I needed this?"

"Ha. We all did after that kid stormed in here with all that attitude."

"I don't like him," Audrey said from the couch.

"Audrey, you don't like anyone," Amanda returned with a funny smile.

"True. But especially him. He's got this 'I'm so troubled, woe is me' vibe, which I can't stand. I remember kids like him in high school. They were such outcasts because they wanted to be outcasts," Audrey said.

"I mean, he is really troubled. And he's Scott's son. So I think we have to have a little more understanding. The world makes fun of him and tears him apart. Probably, he's just built up a lot of boundaries and walls," Susan tried.

Christine sat on the floor near Audrey's feet. She pressed her palms together and nodded; her eyes were far away. "I can only speak about how it was for me, being a kind of outcast back in high school. It was not easy, and you think everyone is out to get you."

"But did anything help? Anything that anyone did?" Susan asked.

Christine shook her head. "Honestly, it took me decades to figure out how to get out of that mode."

"Ugh. It's going to be a long road, isn't it?" Susan said.

Nobody knew how to respond. Susan admitted she was beaten; she brought her glass of wine upstairs with her, where she changed into a pair of flannel pajamas and collapsed on the bed. It had now been nearly an entire week since she and Scott had shared a bed. How she craved the warmth of his body and the rise and fall of his chest as he breathed. She loved the thump-thump of his heartbeat when she pressed her ear against him. And when he awoke, sometimes he told her the events of his dreams in a manner that reminded her of an excited young man and not a man in his mid-forties.

* * *

The following morning, Susan called one of Lola's friends, the journalist who had worked on the Marcie Shean case in Boston. Gretchen Conners was a fast-talking journalist from the Midwest who had arrived in Boston ten years previous and taken the newspaper world by storm. When she greeted Susan, she said immediately, "Why don't you tell that little sister of yours to come on back to Boston? Journalism has fallen behind without her here. She was one of my biggest rivals, you know."

Susan grinned into the phone. "I can imagine that, actually. She's quite a spitfire."

"She says she's found happiness on Martha's Vineyard, whatever happiness is," Gretchen said. "Anyway, she also told me that you have a very famous client."

"Yes. Sad to say, that famous client isn't catching any

springtime sunshine here on the Vineyard, considering she's on house arrest."

"Yes. Well. How can I help you? The trial begins soon, so I assume I'll be seeing you quite a bit out here."

"I would love any insights you have, considering you've been following the case from the start," Susan said. "In regard to the boyfriend. I can't get a good read on his social life."

"You know, I interviewed a few people at this burger place he worked at. They were some real shady characters. Not many of them were willing to give me much information," Gretchen said. "They don't tend to trust journalists, you know. Can't understand why." She snorted into the phone.

"I'm guessing they don't have much trust for lawyers, either," Susan returned.

"Especially since you're trying to prove the apparent accused didn't do it," Gretchen said. "And from what I can tell, anyone affiliated with the boyfriend isn't too keen on our girl Marcie."

Susan and Gretchen spoke for a number of minutes. Gretchen gave a few references, including information about where to find this burger place, then said she would send over all of her notes. Susan thanked her and then checked the time. She had arranged to meet Marcie again in a half-hour. Her heart pounded against her ribcage as she hustled to her car. She thought about bringing Marcie something from the outside world— something she couldn't get for herself, as she was under house arrest. As she had extra time, she stopped over at the Frosted Delights bakery, where she purchased a maple-glazed donut from a smiling Jennifer Conrad.

"Hope you're doing good these days, Susan! You look healthy as ever," Jennifer said.

Obviously, it was common knowledge that Susan had had that bout of cancer. Sometimes, Susan wished the island wasn't so gossip-centric. Back in Newark, there had been other things to care about than other people's business.

Still, it was cozy, knowing so many islanders looked out for you.

By noon, Susan found herself again in Marcie Shean's bedroom. She placed two donuts on a small table off to the side. "I thought maybe you'd like a snack." She tried on a smile, which soon fell flat when Marcie didn't return it.

"My appetite is a bit weird these days," Marcie told her. Her cheekbones protruded from her porcelain skin as she folded her arms over her chest.

"Understandable." Susan opened her folder to find a number of questions that she planned to ask Marcie. As she reached for a pen, her eyes found a photograph on the far desk, which showed Marcie and her dead boyfriend— much younger, much happier, and much more alive. Susan pointed her pen at it and asked, "When was that?"

Marcie turned and blinked at the photo. Susan looked for some sense of alarm or sadness or fear, but instead, the girl just said, "He came to the island about five years ago. We went to the Round-the-Island Sailing Competition. He was in love with the boats. He talked about getting rich and having one of our own."

Susan furrowed her brow. It was mesmerizing listening to this girl discuss the man who no longer lived. It was as though she spoke about someone she had met a long time ago and hadn't caught up with lately.

Maybe she'd created a boundary in her mind to protect herself from sadness. It was difficult to say. Susan, too, had created similar boundaries after she had left the island. Her mother's death had nearly destroyed her.

At that moment, there was a crashing sound from downstairs. Susan bolted toward the door and opened it as the sound of a screaming Mr. Shean billowed over the staircase.

"YOU IDIOT! WHERE DID YOU PUT THE REMOTE?"

Susan's heart raced. She yanked herself around to find Marcie, who hadn't fidgeted at all with the sound.

"He gets angry," Marcie said with a shrug.

"Did he throw something?"

"Maybe. Probably the coffee table. He's done it before. If you look closely, one of the legs is connected with duct tape."

Susan shivered. "He's never hit you or your brother, has he?"

"No. It's mostly just verbal. And it's not like I can blame him right now. Our family is under a lot of stress." Marcie shrugged as she lifted her hand toward one of the donuts. Slowly, she ripped off a very small piece and then placed it delicately on her tongue.

"I DON'T KNOW HOW YOU THINK WE CAN LIVE LIKE THIS," Mr. Shean continued to blare downstairs.

"It must be awful, being back in this house after so much time away," Susan said softly. Against her better judgment, she returned the door to the latch and closed it.

"It's not so bad," Marcie said. "At least all the problems paying rent flew out the window with the arrest. Gosh, we were so broke for so long, and we went to bed hungry all the time. He always said he could get us out of the hole we'd dug ourselves, but I wasn't so sure. And now, I guess, he has his own hole to live in. And I have my own, too. Funny how that works, isn't it? You can have every problem together and then suddenly, you're strangers. One living, one dead."

The girl's words traveled in Susan's brain as she drove back toward Oak Bluffs later that afternoon. It grew increasingly unclear to her whether or not she thought Marcie had murdered her boyfriend. In fact, her father's clear violent tendencies hinted toward violence in the daughter, as well. These sorts of behaviors were known to be passed down through families. She knew that well.

But she couldn't give power to this thought. Not with the trial approaching. It barreled toward her.

Chapter Eight

The knock at Susan's office door wasn't Amanda's. Amanda's was loud, purposeful, the kind that demanded Susan's immediate attention. This one was softer, delicate— yet urgent. And when Susan opened the door to find Scott Frampton before her, holding a bouquet of red roses, her smile was electric with shock and excitement. Why had she ever doubted him? He was her knight in shining armor. She had always known deep down that he would mend everything and ensure everything was all right. This was just his way.

"They're beautiful," she breathed as she nestled her nose between the petals.

Scott wore a pair of dark jeans and a dark button-down shirt. One of his large hands nestled against the base of her back as he led her into her office. Once inside, he shut the door closed and pressed her against the door to kiss her properly. It was the kind of kiss that left her woozy, her head spinning and her knees loose. In those moments, she wasn't a criminal defense lawyer or a soon-to-be evil stepmother; she was just Susie, the girl Scott had fallen in love with about thirty years before.

"To what do I owe the honor?" Susan asked as she grinned sheepishly.

Scott's hand held the back of her head. His eyes glowed with love for her. "I've missed you so much."

"I've missed you, too."

Scott heaved a sigh and stepped back. "I told Kellan that I plan to take you out for dinner tonight. A proper date. Are you up for that?"

Susan nodded. "Yes. Of course." She paused, then added, "But if you want Kellan to come, it's really okay."

"No. I think we need some distance from each other. And if fifteen isn't old enough to stay home alone, I don't know what is."

* * *

Susan dressed in a little swanky black dress, which hit her knees and surged down her breasts beautifully. When she appeared downstairs at the Sheridan house to await Scott's pick-up, Audrey wolf-whistled, and Aunt Kerry, who hovered over a big pot of seafood chowder, said, "Hubba, Hubba." Susan rolled her eyes.

"You girls are shameless," she quipped.

"Sorry. Didn't know I stepped into an episode of *America's Next Top Model*," Audrey said.

"Where are you off to?" Aunt Kerry asked. Her spoon clanked against the base of the pot as she stirred.

"Just dinner with Scott."

"He has a lot to make up for, throwing this boy into the mix," Aunt Kerry said.

Susan longed to insist that everything would be all

right— that Kellan wouldn't throw a wrench into her beautiful plans. But at the moment, she wasn't so sure, and she didn't want to seem foolish. She shrugged and said, "Whatever will be, will be, right?"

"Kind of the Sheridan motto at this point," Audrey agreed, as Baby Max wrapped a hand around her finger and tugged hard.

Scott arrived at the Sheridan house a moment later. He hustled up the steps as Susan entered the warm May evening, and his eyes swelled at the sight of her beauty. When he stepped toward her, his cologne wafted over her, and something in her stomach tightened with excitement. His hand dropped to the base of her back as he stepped closer to her.

"Are you sure you don't want to just stay in?" Scott asked with a smile.

"And waste this dress? No way," Susan replied with a wicked grin.

Scott drove them toward Edgartown, where he parked the truck just south of the Italian restaurant called Cacciapaglia's. They walked hand-in-hand up the sidewalk, passing by several Edgartown socialites, including Mila, who owned the esthetician salon which Susan had begun to frequent.

"Looking radiant, Susan Sheridan," Mila said as she passed.

"All thanks to you, Mila."

"No. This is all thanks to God himself. I just tend to the beautiful garden," Mila said with a wink.

Once at the table, Scott couldn't take his eyes off her. "It's funny, seeing all the people of the Vineyard look at you the way they do. For years, I knew that I had lost something special when you went away, and now that I have you back, I spend most of the time pinching myself. I don't know what on earth I did right to bring you back. But here you are, and I'm totally in love."

They held hands across the white tablecloth as they ordered expensive wine, olives, and cheese to start. The conversation between them flowed beautifully, just as it always had; every few minutes, however, Susan felt stabbed with the memory of Kellan and all the confusion that came with him.

After they ordered their mains— spaghetti and meatballs and lasagna— Susan found herself weaving toward the topic of the wedding, which they had decided long ago would be an outdoor wedding, reserved at the Highfield Hall & Garden on June 19.

"Amanda wants to kill me because I haven't picked out a dress yet," she said. "You've ordered your tux already, haven't you?"

Scott turned his eyes toward the olives. Susan's heart hammered with apprehension.

"I'm sorry. I meant to do that on the day I heard from Kellan's mother. Everything kind of flew out the window after that."

"It's understandable," Susan said hurriedly.

"Yeah. I hope so. I mean, I don't even know how logical any of this is."

"Logical?"

"Yeah."

"What do you mean, exactly?"

"I mean, Kellan just arrived. He's already struggling with school. There are a million things up in the air right now, and I have to relearn how to be a dad..."

Susan leaned back in her chair and released her hand from Scott's. Her lips were downturned.

Scott ran his fingers through his hair and sighed. "I'm sorry. I really am. I find myself not sleeping well. I'm missing you all the time, and I'm terrified that I've already messed up my son because I didn't move to Boston when they did. I feel that I've done so many things wrong. And even now, I'm doing more things wrong. I know you're angry with me. I can feel it. But I don't know how to fix any of this."

Susan's nostrils flared. She'd never seen Scott like this — so whiny, so resistant.

"I don't know what you want me to say. Do you want me to say that we should push back the wedding?"

Scott's eyes widened. "No! I didn't say that."

"I mean, you clearly have some reservations about everything. It's understandable. It's not like I don't have reservations, too. This whole thing was just sprung upon me. I hardly know Kellan, but this version of him is frankly the polar opposite of last year. Not saying that's anyone's fault. Teenagers tend to change in the blink of an eye. I'm just saying. I don't feel fully equipped to deal with him all the time. And I had no idea that I would just suddenly have to play full-time stepmom. You know?"

This was difficult territory. Susan wasn't entirely sure how they'd arrived here. Sure, they'd needed to talk directly since Kellan's arrival. But this wasn't the time nor the place. Already, due to her tone, several other diners had glanced their way in annoyance. Nobody liked a public argument.

"If you need to take a step back from me, from us, then I understand," Scott said somberly.

"I didn't say that. Did I say that?" Susan closed her eyes tight as she swam through her thoughts.

She loved him. She loved him so deeply.

But they had never used such dark words with one another. Not since Susan had left Scott and the island and everything she'd ever known. She wished she could remember exactly what that conversation had been like. Probably, there had been just as much vitriol.

Their main courses arrived. Susan placed her fork into the spaghetti and twirled it round and round and round. Scott ate slowly and quietly. After three bites of her spaghetti, Susan called for the waiter to box up the rest of her meal. She looked at Scott with an icy gaze and said, "I think I'm going to go home."

Scott's shoulders slumped. "Please, don't."

"I just don't know what to do. I don't know if you still want to marry me. I don't know where your head is at. And frankly, I have too much work and too much to deal with, including the Inn and my family, to listen to you waffle from one decision to the next."

Susan took the box of spaghetti from the waiter once he returned, then grabbed her light jacket and stepped toward the door. By the time she reached the curb, an Uber driver had appeared before her, ready to drive her back home. Of course, the Uber driver was someone she'd gone to high school with who couldn't wait to "catch up." Susan tried her best to dig through the conversation, even as her voice threatened to break.

It was only when she got out of the car over in Oak Bluffs that she fully burst into tears.

At that moment, three dark figures appeared at the edge of the woods that stretched around the Sheridan house. Susan peered through the gray light of the late evening. She stepped toward them but teetered slightly as her heels couldn't take the softness of the spring ground.

"Mom? Is that you?" Amanda hustled out from the

tree line as the others, Grandpa Wes and Audrey, who had a sleeping Max strapped to her chest, stepped lightly behind.

Susan dropped her chin onto her daughter's shoulder as she exhaled somberly. She shook against her as Amanda's hand rubbed her upper back.

In a moment, Wes appeared beside them— the tall, still-powerful patriarch of the family. He wrapped his arms around them and then drew Audrey in as they joined in a huddle. After a moment of beautiful silence, Susan asked, "What were you four doing out in the woods?"

"Watching for birds, of course," Audrey said. "Before Max fell asleep, he saw quite a few spectacular ones. Grandpa Wes is already trying to turn him into a big, bird-watching nerd, like him."

"Rude, Audrey," Wes said with a big smile.

"Let's go inside. We'll make some hot chocolate," Amanda said. "It suddenly got very chilly out here."

"It's not summer yet. That's for sure," Wes affirmed.

Back inside, Susan slipped into her flannel pajamas and sat on the couch between Audrey and Wes. Max slept peacefully upstairs while Amanda boiled water and stirred up delicious hot cocoa. The television delivered a sterling set of romantic comedies, including *Trainwreck* and *How to Lose a Guy in Ten Days*, and Susan dug herself deeper into the couch and listened to the tender laughter of Amanda and Audrey. Wes's soft snores came only a few minutes into the first movie, and Amanda hustled to grab his hot cocoa mug before he spilled the piping hot liquid over his lap.

"We take care of each other here," Amanda said primly as she placed the mug on the counter. She then gave her mother heavy eye contact as she added, "And we don't need anyone else."

Oh, but Susan knew in her heart of hearts that while she didn't need Scott, she loved him dearly. They would surely find a way through this horrible fight. She just felt a bit hopeless at the moment. It would pass. Every bad feeling always found a way out.

Chapter Nine

The day before the trial of the State Versus Marcie Shean, Susan and Amanda piled into Susan's car, armed with six very thick stacks of legal notes Susan had gathered for the approaching trial and two whopping cups of black coffee. The sun dimmed over the eastern horizon line and cast the Vineyard in a strange, overcast light. "I haven't been awake this early in a while," Amanda breathed. "Hard to believe I used to wake up at five every day to do Pilates just to get ahead of my to-do list."

"You're a monster," Susan said with a laugh.

"I've gotten better at it and much looser. Audrey says that I'm not as tightly wound as I used to be," Amanda said. "I always tell her she could do with a few wounds up. But she seems to be taking the whole motherhood thing in stride."

"She's a natural. I know she was terrified these last few months. And it'll be interesting to see how she handles going back to Penn State in the fall. If someone

A Vineyard Wedding

had told me I had to leave you or Jake after you'd been born, I would have torn them apart."

Amanda grimaced. "I still hope she goes. She wants to be a journalist so badly, and there are just things about being on campus you can't get back after you've missed the window. Max won't remember. And she'll still be allowed this whole other life."

Susan drove the car up the ramp of the ferry and slipped easily into a parking spot within the belly of the boat. Once parked, they slipped out of the car and headed up to the seating area, with its illustrious view of the water. Only three other people were on board, as six in the morning wasn't exactly a common time for Vineyard departure. Amanda and Susan wanted to get a head-start on the day and get their heads in line for the beginning of the trial. Susan sizzled with adrenaline.

Once they'd sat down, Susan's phone pinged.

> SCOTT: Hey. The other night was such a mess. If you find the time while you're away, please call me. I would love to explain more about what I'm thinking.

Susan darkened the phone instead of answering. She then turned her head as the ferry pulled away from the island. The motor made everything purr and vibrate, including the coffee in her paper cup. Susan's eyes found Amanda's.

"You still haven't talked to him?" Amanda asked.

Susan shrugged. "I texted him yesterday to tell him my schedule for the week, but honestly, he needs space to deal with this Kellan situation. Maybe we should push off the wedding. I don't know."

Amanda scrunched her nose. "I hate that all this is happening."

Susan patted her heart. "The only thing I want to care about right now is Marcie Shean. We have a job to do in Boston, and we have to reserve our hearts and souls for it. I know you haven't had a lot of experience out in the field like this, so I hope you take this all in. It will be difficult and emotional and probably very strange. But I know we can handle it."

Susan prayed she would soon believe her own words.

The drive up to Boston was unceremonious. When they spotted the skyline, Susan reached back and grabbed a manila folder, which she placed on Amanda's lap. "I want to drive by the house where it happened. The address should be on the third page found in this folder. Can you type it into Maps?"

Amanda did as she was told and then guided her mother toward the dank and divey streets where Marcie and the man she had loved had once lived. Redbrick buildings stretched on either side of the vehicle as Susan slowed. It was just past nine in the morning, and the city bustled with morning action. Pedestrians burst out onto the road, holding Dunkin Donuts coffees, their eyes glowing with a sense of mission and importance.

"Such a different energy than the island," Amanda said. "It's possible I've been on the Vineyard too long."

"You've become an Islander now. All other life feels foreign," Susan said. "I feel the same way."

Amanda flung a hand forward then and cried, "Look! That's their building number. Park here."

Susan slotted her car off to the right and turned off the engine. When she stood out on the sidewalk before the house, she tried her best to feel the heinous crime in the air around the place. In truth, though, the house just looked like any old house. The neighbors who passed by looked typical, nondescript. Nothing about the place gave off an air of mystery.

"Hard to believe it all happened here," Amanda said, echoing Susan's thoughts.

"True." When Susan turned her head, she found herself peering at the precise place where that now-famous photo of Marcie had been taken. There, on that very piece of sidewalk, the girl had been terrified beyond any earthly understanding— regardless of whether or not she had committed the crime.

Susan and Amanda set themselves up at the downtown hotel located closest to the courthouse, where the trial was set to begin the following day. They worked primly and properly, both overwhelmingly organized, and soon fell into a rhythm of the last elements they needed to check up on. Amanda passed over the last edits she'd done of Susan's opening statement, which Susan blinked at ruefully. Was this really her best effort? She had worked on it tirelessly over the previous few days, yet it still seemed to miss some kind of magical element.

"You're doubting it," Amanda said.

"No. I mean. Kind of."

Amanda heaved a sigh. "I knew it. You're a perfectionist."

"But can you see if I should add anything else?"

"No. I told you. I think it's really strong," Amanda replied.

Around three in the afternoon, Susan's stomach quaked with hunger. "I think I'd like to go eat at the burger place the boyfriend worked at."

Amanda arched an eyebrow. "Gretchen said to check up with those guys, didn't she?"

"Yeah."

"And you're sure it isn't dangerous?" Amanda asked.

Susan shrugged. "It's in public. We'll just go in as unsuspecting burger eaters. Nothing more."

"It's been a long time since I had a decent burger," Amanda admitted.

Susan parked the car in the back lot of the burger place. Outside, the air steamed with smells of sizzling burgers and fries. They entered through a side door and found themselves in the midst of a super-hip establishment, with countless framed portraits on the walls of sports teams and celebrities; graffiti covered nearly every surface, and the servers all seemed lazy but cool, the kinds who talked your ear off but usually forgot your order.

"How ya'll doing today?" the guy who greeted them had a southern accent, which was strange in the midst of so much Boston.

"Great, thanks."

"Booth? Bar? What works for you ladies today?"

"Bar, please." Susan wanted to be in an area where they could potentially see everything and ask questions if needed.

The host walked them up to the bar, where they sat on two stools and pored over the sticky menus. Both Susan and Amanda ordered iced tea, which the bartender gathered promptly.

"What can I grab you ladies to eat?" the bartender asked as he slid two drink coasters beneath their cold drinks.

"I'll have the bacon cheeseburger," Susan said.

"And I'll have the chicken burger," Amanda returned.

"Let's share onion rings?"

"And fries."

"I can mix those up for you," the bartender said. "Not a problem."

Susan and Amanda made heavy eye contact as they clinked their glasses together. There was a whole lot to cheer for and a whole lot to hope for. Susan sizzled with adrenaline, as she always did when she attempted to mold together a legal case. She had a strange itch to call Richard and explain what she was up to since they'd previously done so much of this together. Now, Amanda was her partner. A funny yet beautiful switch.

The bartender hovered near them after that and flipped through the channels to find another sport. "Midday sports are a bit weird," he explained. "Normally, it's like, pool or cards or something like that. Just background noise. Maybe we could do the news?"

This triggered something in the back of Susan's mind.

"Yeah! The news sounds great," Susan said. "Good to stay up-to-date."

"I feel the same, but I have to admit, I haven't been so good about it lately," the bartender said. He snapped on the local news, which was in the midst of a local traffic report. "Great. I can't wait to see the weather woman. I have a crush on her."

Susan laughed good-naturedly and settled in. It was surely only a matter of time before the Marcie Shean case would spring to life on the screen. Then, she could dig her teeth in.

Their French fry-onion ring combo came out before their burgers. Amanda lifted one greasy circle to the light and said, "This is a masterpiece." The bartender laughed outright and said, "I knew I liked you girls."

Susan flashed Amanda a wide grin. This sort of thing just came naturally to Amanda, it seemed. This pleased her a lot.

As Susan snuck her teeth over a fry, the news finally changed. The words splayed across the screen: **TOMORROW BEGINS MARCIE SHEAN MURDER TRIAL**.

The bartender whistled as his shoulders sagged. The news showed video footage of Marcie being taken out of the very house they had seen that day, in handcuffs and covered in blood.

"You guys know about this, right?" the bartender said.

"A little bit," Susan offered.

"Actually, I have friends who knew them," Amanda piped up. "Didn't the guy work here?"

The bartender heaved a sigh and stretched a hand behind his head. He nodded ever-so-slightly and then pressed a finger to his lips. "It's a bit awkward to talk about. The boss doesn't want us advertising it. But you know, you girls are some of the only people in here, so, anyway. Yeah. The vile devil worked here."

Susan's eyebrows popped up. "So, you didn't like him so much?"

The bartender shrugged. "I don't know. He used to be a good guy, a great guy, even. But something changed over the past few years." He leaned heavily against the bar and turned his eyes back toward the screen. "He and Marcie were perfect together for a while. I was super jealous of him. Marcie was so beautiful and so sweet, you know? But you could tell there was some serious trouble brewing between them. And you heard stories about some violence between them. But then again, he was into some pretty weird stuff. At least, that's what I heard."

"Weird stuff? What do you mean?" Susan asked.

"Well, I mean. He and Marcie were always pinching pennies. And I heard that he got himself involved with some bad people to try to make some more money for them."

"Like what? Drugs?" Amanda asked.

"Drugs, maybe. Some kind of smuggling? I don't know. I try to keep on the straight and narrow myself. But his personality sure did change that last year before he died. If she didn't do it— which, I know, all of Boston believes she did— then it has to be one of those druggy dudes he was working with. But I don't know. I'm no expert. I just know that it would be a tragedy if that beautiful girl ended up behind bars for good."

Chapter Ten

Back at the hotel, Amanda was a boisterous ball of energy. She jumped on the bed and cried, "I can't believe he just gave us all that information! He had no idea what we were up to!"

Susan chewed her lower lip contemplatively. Slowly, she removed her sweater, then donned a camisole and a pair of flannel pajama pants. Outside, a siren blared ominously. In only twelve hours, she would meet Marcie Shean on the morning of the first day of her murder trial. Everything hinged on the final work she could do that night. It would set the tone for the entire trial.

"I think I'm going to rewrite my opening statement," Susan said suddenly.

Amanda's jaw dropped. She stepped off the bed, then dropped herself on edge. "Why? It's perfect. You're crazy if you do."

"I'm not. We learned too much today for me not to incorporate some of it. And after what the bartender told us, we have a whole lot more digging to do. We need to track down people who either know these drug dealers or smugglers or people who understand what the boyfriend was doing with them. I don't know how much Marcie knows about all of this. Maybe she's kept this under wraps because she was a part of it and doesn't want to get into trouble?"

"I think selling drugs is a whole lot better than murdering your boyfriend," Amanda pointed out.

"Sure. But she was scared. Maybe she lied at first and then had to stand with the lie to make sure that nobody pointed to her wishy-washy testimony as proof that she killed him."

Amanda buzzed her lips. She then rose up from the bed and began to pace. "You sure you want to stay up and write this thing? You'll want to be fresh tomorrow."

"I'll be fine," Susan said. "I work better with adrenaline, and besides, it won't take long. I know I have to be fresh for tomorrow morning, which means I'll need my sleep."

Susan sat at the desk while Amanda headed into the bathroom to draw herself a bath. Susan's fingers began to type frantically; her thoughts raced as the words fell across the page. When she came to, she realized that Amanda had been out of the bath for so long that she'd fallen asleep in her robe on top of the covers of her bed. Susan's heart swelled with motherly love. She stepped toward her daughter and pressed a hand against her shoulder. Amanda jumped slightly, then became heavy against the mattress again.

"What happened?" Amanda asked dreamily.

"You passed out with a towel wrapped around your hair," Susan said with a smile. "You know that'll mess up your look tomorrow."

"Too true," Amanda affirmed. Slowly, she stepped up

from the mattress and returned to the bathroom. After a moment, there was the warm roar of the hairdryer.

Susan continued to type as Amanda fell into a deep sleep as the night ticked on. She felt frantic yet sure of herself, a strange combination that reminded her of long-ago days when she'd forced herself through late-night papers, even while her babies were young. She had nearly destroyed herself to get through law school. Richard hadn't exactly been marvelous help in the father department. Men never really realized how much work it took.

* * *

At eight the following morning, Susan and Amanda stepped into one of the side offices at the courthouse to meet with Marcie. The girl was dressed primly in a high-collared lace dress, which Susan had actually picked out for her. She had her hands folded over her lap, which highlighted the soft pink color of her nails. Her hair was pinned back, which made her look youthful and intelligent, so unlike the wild beauty from the photograph.

Beside Marcie sat her father and her brother, both of whom wore gray suits. Not one of them smiled. On the far end of the room, two guards stood with their hands behind their backs.

"Good morning," Susan said to Marcie. "How was your trip to Boston?"

Marcie nodded. "It was good to get off the island. First time in a long time."

"I bet." Susan's heart pounded. She then gestured toward Amanda to say, "This is my assistant."

Marcie turned a sharp eye. "You're practically twins."

"She's also my daughter," Susan added. "Good eye."

A Vineyard Wedding

"Strong genes," Marcie said. "I look just like my mother, too. Dad hates it."

Beside her, her father shifted strangely and turned his eyes toward the door. Susan couldn't begin to stab through the tension in the room. It was overwhelming.

It was time to enter the courtroom. Susan and Amanda weaved their way to their assigned seats, across the aisle from the boyfriend's lawyer. Behind the lawyer sat the boyfriend's family: a mother and father and a brother who looked just like him. Susan's stomach twisted. It was difficult to think of them and all the pain and torment this caused them. There would be so much evidence brought to the courtroom that would make them sick.

She prayed that she would never go through anything like this.

It was hell on earth.

Then, the guards led Marcie in to be seated alongside Susan. Behind them sat the father and brother. Susan witnessed Marcie as she turned the slightest bit to catch sight of the boyfriend's family. Her cheeks turned so white that they were almost blue. Susan didn't need her to faint. Not then.

It was announced that it was time for opening statements. The prosecutor stood from his bench and buttoned his suit jacket. He then stepped toward the center of the courtroom to address the jury.

Susan had heard of this lawyer before. Paul Soloman. He was cut-throat and intelligent. You could feel it in everything he did. Even his suit was a stellar cut for his body shape; his hair seemed the perfect amount of black and gray, a beautiful salt and pepper. His voice was smooth and deep— the kind you could trust.

"May it please the court? Counsel. Ladies and gentlemen of the jury, good morning. My name is Paul Soloman, and I am here to discuss a horrific crime— a crime of such despicable nature that it's difficult to name and comprehend. In this case, you will learn that on November 13, Marcie Shean murdered her boyfriend, Freddy Peterson, in cold blood. They had a volatile relationship, one that several members of their friend group and social circle and even family can attest to."

The opening statement continued on for several more minutes. Paul Soloman discussed the beauty of young love, which is so easily crushed by the sands of time. He suggested that Marcie was intoxicated and angry and even mentioned his knowledge that she came from a rather violent family. Susan stirred with anxiety but kept her spine pin-straight. This would be fine. It would all be fine.

Finally, it was her turn. Susan stood and marched toward the center of the courtroom. She, too, buttoned her suit jacket and then lifted her chin. In this strange moment, as countless eyes and video cameras turned toward her, she was reminded of how much she had gone through over the previous year. She'd kicked cancer's butt, for crying out loud.

Now, she had a chance to save this poor girl's life. She couldn't screw it up.

"Ladies and gentlemen of the jury. Counsel. My name is Susan Sheridan, and I am here to discuss something called reasonable doubt. Throughout every element of the case and the evidence that is put forth by the prosecution, I need you to understand that on that fateful day, November 13, when Freddy Peterson was taken from this world— not a single soul in this room saw what happened.

A Vineyard Wedding

The only person who knows what happened on that fateful day that we know of is Freddy Peterson himself. Freddy left this world in a way that was wholly unfair and entirely evil.

"The only person in this world who knew Freddy very well over the previous years was the defendant. The defendant has been labeled a cruel vixen, an evil woman, and a person without a moral compass. But these are just words and baseless statements blared across news channels. These are words that sell newspapers and magazines. They have nothing at all to do with this very human, very kind, very gentle young woman you see before you— a woman who loved her boyfriend more than we can possibly imagine.

"I don't know about any of you, but I remember what it was like to be young and in love. It had a whole different range of hardships because everything was on the line. You're worried about where you're going in life. You're worried about whether or not you've chosen the correct partner. You're worried, and you're in love, and you're aching all over. And for this reason, you fight— a lot.

"But just because you fight doesn't mean your mind heads to that dark, horrible place of murder. We've all fought and broken up and ached without killing our partners in cold blood, haven't we? And here is where I begin to build your reasonable doubt. There is simply not enough feasible evidence to conclude that Marcie Shean killed Freddy Peterson that day."

Susan's opening statement continued for a number of minutes. As she spoke, she felt the jury's heavy gazes upon her; she sensed that she captivated every soul within the room. And when she sat down on the wooden bench again, Amanda gripped her hand and gave her an earnest smile.

"That was fantastic, Mom. I'm glad you rewrote it."

Susan's heart swelled with excitement. They would find a way through this. They had to.

Chapter Eleven

Amanda drove Susan's car all the way back to Martha's Vineyard to allow Susan more time to go through her case notes. Susan sat in the backseat, covered in documents and files, her laptop propped open to the right and her pen poised over a pad of paper. Susan hardly noticed the trek back and only realized how close they were when she felt the thump-thump of the tires against the ramp as they headed up onto the ferry.

"How are you doing back there, Erin Brockovich?" Amanda teased as she eased into one of the parking spots in the boat itself.

"Phew. I lost my head there for a while." Susan placed a stack of papers off to the side and then stretched her arms through the air so that her shoulders cracked.

"Let's go have a glass of wine up on top," Amanda said. "It's still a beautiful day. And I think we need it."

As Amanda ordered chardonnay for the both of them, Susan sat at one of the small, round tables which lined the café area on the ferry. This was the first chance she'd had to check her phone, and when she did, there was an outpouring of messages.

> CHRISTINE: Good luck today, Big Sis! Lola and I want to have a BBQ to celebrate Day One.

> LOLA: BBQ tonight! Everyone's invited!

> AUDREY: I hope you make all my favorite legal crime shows proud today, Aunt Susan! Also, I'm bragging about you to all my college friends. And also to Max, but he can't understand yet.

> SCOTT: Hey babe! Good luck today. I was thinking about you so much.

> SCOTT: Christine and Lola told me about the BBQ. I hate to do this, but I can't go. Kellan has a big meeting tonight with some of his teachers, and I need to be there.

> SCOTT: I feel like a total failure for not being there tonight. I'll try to stop by afterward if you want that.

> SCOTT: Love you so much, Susan.

Susan groaned as she read the last of Scott's words. Amanda sat across from her and tapped her glass of wine before her. When Susan looked up, she scrunched her nose and said, "I guess you already know about this big celebration at the house?"

Amanda nodded. "But I only just learned. Lola and Christine love doing these. I hope you're not too tired.

Nobody knows how much work you put into today. I kind of do, but I slept through the night. You didn't."

"I'll be fine, I'm sure," Susan said. "I just wanted more time to go over the case tonight.

"I'm sure everyone will understand if you need to step away to prep," Amanda said. "You know that they just want an excuse to eat together."

* * *

Back at the Sheridan house, a BBQ was already in full swing. Tommy Gasbarro hovered over the grill, in Scott's normal position, and flipped burgers and BBQ chicken. Lola had hung streamers across the porch, and Christine blared old nineties tunes from a portable speaker, which she had placed on the other side of the porch. Grandpa Wes sat with a beer, his eyes toward the horizon line on the glittering Vineyard Sound, and Audrey made funny faces at baby Max, who, she said, needed to learn what "funny" meant before he learned anything else.

"He's my son. He needs to know how to banter," she affirmed to everyone. "And it all starts with facial mannerisms."

"What if he grows up and he's not funny?" Amanda asked as she stepped toward the other table, where Lola had placed a number of chips and chopped veggies. "What if he wants to be a serious politician? Or a chess master? Or..."

Audrey arched an eyebrow at Amanda. "Or what if he wants to grow up like his Aunt Amanda, Type A to the core?"

Amanda's grin widened. "Would that be such a bad

thing? Maybe he could help you stay organized. Tell you when to change the kitchen sponge or—"

Audrey scoffed and then made another playful face for Max. "Max, are you really going to be an organized, boring person? Or you wanna be like your mom? Fiery with a sense of crazy!"

"Oh, great. Another generation done for." Amanda chuckled as she layered celery and carrots onto her plate. She gestured toward Audrey as she added, "Do you want me to make a plate of veggies for you?"

At this, Audrey, who'd basically already bounced back to her pre-baby body, shook her head. "Are you kidding? It's a BBQ. I want fatty food and meat."

At this, Amanda rolled her eyes yet continued to laugh.

Lola appeared beside Susan and wrapped an arm around her. "You look tired, Susie. How did it go today?"

"I have to admit. I'm beat," Susan said. "Although we had a good opening day. Marcie seems a bit freaked out, but I guess that's to be expected."

"Poor girl," Christine offered from the other side of the porch swing, where she sat with her head on Grandpa Wes's shoulder.

"Do you think she did it?" Wes asked Susan then.

Susan was surprised at the question. She slid a strand of hair behind her ear and gave him a half-smile. "It doesn't matter, really. I just have to put a seed of doubt into the mind of the jury."

"So she did do it," Wes interjected.

"No, not necessarily, Grampa. There's definitely some unsubstantiated evidence that is obvious. Her prints are all over the place because it's her apartment, for God's sake," Amanda stated. "It's a complex case."

"Everyone I talk to seems to think she murdered the poor guy in cold blood," Wes said. "But you know how people are. They get these opinions in their heads."

Susan thought it was mildly funny that Wes sat around with others discussing the very case that had suddenly and totally taken over her life.

Tommy announced that the burgers and chicken were ready. Together, they sat around the table— Zach, Christine, Audrey, Grandpa Wes, Lola, Tommy, Susan, and Amanda. As Lola smeared some mayonnaise on her burger bun, she blinked up and asked, "Scott said he couldn't make it. We were disappointed."

"Yeah. Another Kellan obligation, I guess," Susan said as brightly as she could, even as her heart dipped lower in her belly. "Makes total sense. It's a huge undertaking, moving high schools. None of our kids ever had to do it, thankfully."

Lola made a soft noise in her throat. Her eyes turned toward Christine as though they now shared a thought together, one that required no vocalization. Susan would have maybe called them out, but her head panged with fatigue.

"Well, in any case, we have a number of ideas for the wedding, if you have some time for it," Lola said finally, just before she took an enormous bite of her burger.

"We'll find time," Susan answered. She then placed her half-eaten burger on her plate and turned her face toward the screen door. Everything within her screamed to get back to work; Marcie Shean relied on her. She couldn't very well spend all these moments enjoying life, not with so much on the line.

Susan finally made an excuse and stepped into the house. Once there, she entered the room that Amanda had claimed after the failed wedding back in January. The room definitely had a "This is Amanda's Space" feel to it. It was incredibly organized, crisp, and the bed was always made in a way that reminded Susan of a *Home and Gardens* magazine. Susan sat at Amanda's desk and placed her computer and a large folder before her. She would remain there until Amanda wanted the room back— and then she'd head back upstairs and do the rest of the work from bed.

The Sheridans out on the porch continued to laugh and joke and banter into the night. Susan used earplugs at some point to ensure that she could remain focused. Just past eleven at night, she checked her phone and was surprised to see that Scott Frampton, of all people, had written her.

> SCOTT: I'm headed to your house. Will you meet me for a little walk along the water?

Susan furrowed her brow. The message had been sent about ten minutes before, which probably meant that Scott was already there. She grabbed her jacket and rushed through the living room, then decided to head out the back way and scoop around the porch to avoid any questions from her loving but prying family members. They meant well. They always did.

Scott sat toward the line of trees, off to the right of the dock that snuck into the water, on which they had latched Scott's speedboat only a few days before, in pursuit of some idea of spring. Scott gazed out across the water; he'd collected himself on top of a stump, and his hair caught the breeze off the water beautifully. He looked thoughtful, masculine. Susan could have watched him like that for a long time. How hungry she felt to know his inner thoughts.

"Scott. Hi." Susan appeared beside him and wrapped a strand of hair around her ear. Her heart seemed to pulse in her throat.

His eyes found hers. They echoed with love, the forever kind. He stood and wrapped his thick arms around her and held her like that, without speaking, for nearly a full minute. Susan thought back to the opening statement she'd made earlier that day. How terrified she had been! This moment of safety was a complete contrast to that.

Scott beckoned for her to sit with him on the stump. She did and placed her hands on her knees. She felt like a little kid. Above them, the moon was huge and cast a bright glow across the water.

"I'm so proud of you, Susan Sheridan," Scott said. "You were always the smartest woman I'd ever known. And now, the world's eyes are upon you."

"It's a strange feeling. Especially because the whole thing was so rushed," Susan admitted. "I want to make sure I give this girl all I can. She deserves that much at least."

Scott nodded. His large hand wrapped over hers. It was warm, powerful, and strong. It almost overwhelmed Susan.

"It's been quite a time, hasn't it?" Scott breathed. "Only a couple of weeks since Kellan arrived. And now, you're full-throttle into this trial, and I'm going to parent-teacher meetings."

A lump formed in Susan's throat. She knew what needed to be asked, even if she didn't want to do it.

"What do you need right now?" she finally asked. "What do you need from me? From our relationship?"

Scott's eyes dropped toward the ground. "I don't know. I guess I just need your patience as I figure this next chapter out."

Susan nodded, even as tears sprung to her eyes. "Do you think we should push back the wedding? I feel crazy asking since it's only a month away. But here we are."

"I just don't know."

Susan nodded. This information was essential. It showed her where they stood.

But now what?

"We have to decide soon," she said. "It's not the end of the world if it doesn't happen this summer."

Even as she said it, her heart felt cracked. Scott held her gaze for a moment. His thumb traced a line along her palm.

"I have to get back to the case," she finally said. "Get home safe, okay?" She kissed his cheek gently and then headed back around the side of the house. Once back at Amanda's desk, she only allowed herself to cry for a few minutes. After that, she directed her attention back to the case.

She was Susan Sheridan. She could withstand this heartbreak. This was just another confusing element in a confusing yet completely blessed life.

Chapter Twelve

The following morning was Saturday. Susan rolled over beneath the scratchy comforter of the upstairs bed and peered out of the window, which caught the full rush of pink buds from the nearest tree. On the far end of the bed still sat a number of court documents, research, and notes from her long night of work; her head remained fuzzy from all the work she had done the previous night. Maybe, at forty-five, all of this was a bit too torturous on her. Maybe she needed to take a step back.

That moment, the door sprung open. Audrey and Amanda barreled in, acting like silly teenagers.

"Aunt Susie!"

"Mom!"

"We have a surprise for you!"

"Get up! Now!"

"Allez!" Amanda cried in French as she grabbed her mother's hand and tugged gently.

Susan rubbed her eye as her groan turned into a laugh. "All right. All right. I'll get up."

Amanda drew open the closet and selected a dark blue dress and a pair of modest heels. She then said, "You have a half-hour to get ready and then the car is headed out of the driveway, Missy. Step on it."

"The student becomes the master," Susan said mid-yawn. "All right. I'll make it happen. Now scram, so I can jump in the shower."

When Susan appeared downstairs, she found Lola, Christine, Amanda, and Audrey all waiting for her. Max slept in his baby carrier when Audrey said, "He can sleep through anything. Trains. Loud screaming. Grandpa Wes's snores."

"Hey! I heard that." Grandpa Wes stepped out of the little breakfast nook area with a cup of coffee in his hand. He grinned at them as he ruffled his gray curls. "Look at my girls, all of you together. Where are you off to?"

"It's a surprise, Dad," Lola answered with a wide grin. "And oh look! Aunt Kerry is here."

Aunt Kerry stepped into the house and hollered hello. Once she reached Wes, she formed a fist and bumped it against his bicep. "You ready for me to beat you in a round of cards, Brother?"

"My babysitter is back again," Wes said, teasing both Kerry and himself. He knew that he couldn't be left at home alone; he knew it was for his benefit. Plus, Kerry was one of his very favorite people, so he didn't mind much.

Grandpa Wes called for them all to have fun as they piled into two cars— Christine's and Lola's. Susan sat up front in Christine's, with Audrey and Max in the back, while Amanda headed over with Lola. Often, Susan wondered what Lola and Amanda spoke about when they were alone together, as the two were just about as different as any two creatures. Still, as they jumped out of the car over in Edgartown, they were in the midst of uproarious laughter. It warmed Susan's heart just as much as it confused her.

In Edgartown, the five of them, plus Baby Max, headed into the Frosted Delights Bakery. They ordered a wide selection of delightful donuts and sat around a table to people-watch and gossip. Jennifer Conrad and her mother were both stationed behind the counter, which was thrilling to witness, as Jennifer's mother had had a horrific stroke back in December. This event had led to Jennifer taking over the bakery, despite her blossoming career as a social media manager. This reminded Susan of herself: this constant drive to take over everything, even beyond time constraints. Jennifer, in contrast to Susan, had recently divorced her high school sweetheart and became involved with a high-powered developer from New York City. It was funny where life took you.

Susan ate one-half of a chocolate-glazed donut with a hazelnut cream filling, then rolled her eyes back in her head. "This is insanely delicious." She waved to Jennifer over the counter and called, "You keep outdoing yourself!"

Jennifer laughed. "My mom is obsessed with inventing new recipes. You would think after working here for over forty years, she would have had enough, but I guess not!"

When Susan returned her attention to her table, they looked at her mischievously. They had already gathered up the rest of her half-donut, along with the uneaten pieces they'd ordered, and announced that they would eat the rest of the donuts after the real surprise.

"What the heck?" Susan asked as she followed them out into the light sunshine of the May morning.

The girls led her down the street, back toward a little white house with long floor-to-ceiling windows and a large willow tree out front.

"What is this place?" she asked.

Amanda tugged her hand as she guided her up the little path. Once at the door, they rang the bell; a second later, a woman of about seventy, wearing cat-eyeglasses, appeared in the doorway. She beamed at Susan as she said, "This must be the beautiful bride."

Susan's heart drummed with confusion. She hadn't had time to discuss any of her and Scott's conversation from the previous night with her sisters or her daughter—and thusly, they'd crafted a surprise that had something to do with the wedding. As she stepped into the house after the older woman, she found herself in a sea of vintage-looking wedding dresses, all of them unique and delicate, all with their own histories and beautiful stories. Susan's eyes immediately welled with sadness.

"Wow," she breathed, feeling the eyes of her sisters upon her. "This is truly spectacular."

"It's something of a hobby of mine," the older woman said. "I collect antique wedding dresses and fix them up and then serve them to the beautiful brides of Martha's Vineyard or whoever wants to travel to see them, of course. Some of them have been used in films; others were used by celebrities long ago. When my husband died, I filled up the entire house with gowns. Maybe hobby is the wrong word. It's more of an obsession."

Susan nearly lost her breath. Amanda roped her arm through Susan's and whispered, "Don't you want to try one? I didn't want you to eat all that donut; I knew you'd kill me if I left you to do that."

Susan tried to laugh, but the sound of it grew lost in her throat. The older woman's eyes bore into her. She had to do something, to at least try one. She pointed toward one in the corner, a cream-colored gown from the forties with a high neckline. It was absolutely stunning, something fit for Old Hollywood. And in a moment, she had the thing over her breasts and buttoned up the back. She stepped out of the dressing room area and stood before a mirror with her two sisters, her daughter, her niece, and the old collector behind her. They *ooohed* and *aahed* at the glorious view, and in truth, Susan couldn't have imagined anything more unique and stunning for her wedding to the love of her life.

But as her thoughts swirled, as Lola squealed, "Oh, Susan, you dreamboat," and as Max suddenly cooed in his little carrier, Susan found herself hunching forward as tears rolled down her cheeks. A sob escaped her throat. The older woman watched in horror as the result of her perfect collection pushed Susan into agony.

Amanda rushed in front of her to collect Susan's head on her shoulder. Susan sobbed again as the older woman grabbed a large towel and placed it beneath Susan's chin.

"I just don't want the fabric to get wet from your tears, dear," she said under her breath.

"I understand!" Susan cried. How pitiful she felt. How weak.

"Mom? What is going on?" Amanda's voice was somber yet warm. She placed a tender hand on Susan's upper shoulder and led her toward the far end of the room, where they sat on a couch.

Christine, Lola, and Audrey followed after them.

Susan gestured toward the dress and said, "This dress deserves a happier occasion."

"What on earth are you talking about?" Lola demanded.

The older woman looked both perturbed and curious. Susan blinked out and said, finally, both terrified and not, that they weren't sure if they needed to push back the wedding. "There's just so much going on. I don't want to pressure Scott into an immediate marriage, especially when he's got his hands full with Kellan."

Lola closed her eyes tight. "It's such bad timing. And it's not your fault!"

"No. It's not. And you know, Scott loves you more than anything," Christine added.

"I know that. I do." Susan gestured down at the dress. "It's just, for the past few months, I've really dreamed about this wedding. I couldn't wait to tell Scott Frampton 'I do' after all these years apart. And now, it doesn't really feel like the dream I always imagined it to be."

Nobody seemed to know what to say. The beautiful plan had backfired, and now, Susan Sheridan— the normal backbone of the entire family had proved herself to be frightened and sad and not at all this "strong woman" Susan herself had perceived herself to be.

"I should really get out of this dress, huh?" Susan finally said, trying to brighten her voice. "I probably look like a bridezilla who just had a serious meltdown."

"You really don't," Christine said then. She whipped around toward the collector and said, "Will you just hold this one off to the side? Just until Susan knows for sure."

The woman drew her hands together gently. Her eyes were rimmed red.

"I can see how much you love him," she said.

Susan nodded as she sniffled again. "I really do. I would wear a paper sack just to marry him."

"But you shouldn't. You should wear this. When you're ready," the woman said. "You look like a classic movie star. So regal. So proud."

Susan was overwhelmed with her feelings. She stood from the sofa and glanced again at her reflection in the mirror. The woman who peered back looked devastated; the woman who peered back wanted to eat the rest of her donut. The woman in the mirror didn't have anything figured out.

"Don't give it away just yet," she told the woman in a whisper. "Thank you."

When she and the girls reappeared outside the wedding dress shop, Susan admitted she had to get back to work. Her sisters and daughter and niece gave her worried smiles. Susan drew her hands up between them and waved them as she said, "Don't worry about me, okay? That was just a small little psychotic break. It's been a strange few weeks. But you know me. I'll come out on top."

"You always do," Lola affirmed. "But we can help you along the way, you know."

"Stubborn Susan Sheridan," Christine said with a crooked smile. "You don't have to be so strong all the time."

Chapter Thirteen

That week, it was decided that they needed to hire another lawyer to maintain the Sheridan Law Office while Susan spent so much time in Boston. They had received a tip from a friend that an islander who'd spent the previous decades in Boston had returned in the wake of his wife's death and was hungry to work for a law firm again. "Apparently, he's fantastic, but he came to the island to live a quieter life, closer to his family," Amanda said as she read through his referrals and his resume again.

Bruce Holland stepped into the Sheridan Law Office Monday afternoon. He was a hunk of a man, even Susan had to admit it— perhaps six foot four, broad-shouldered, with a smile that looked borderline arrogant. Amanda's eyes were buggy as she trailed after him and into Susan's office for the interview. Within the hour, Susan had hired him. Bruce Holland wasn't the type of guy you didn't hire.

With Bruce around, Susan could pass off a few other cases and give herself more space to head off to Boston.

A Vineyard Wedding

She was gone by two in the afternoon— speeding up from Woods Hole all the way back to that beautiful city and the girl within it, Marcie Shean. As she clutched the steering wheel, she tried to imagine what it had been like for Marcie Shean as she'd sprung off the island of Martha's Vineyard and into the rest of her future. What had she dreamed of on that fateful day? Had she had dreams, desires that extended beyond the love she'd found? Had she been hunting for something in particular?

Certainly, she hadn't planned for this.

Susan checked herself back into the same hotel room and arranged the room just so. She texted Amanda throughout to tell her that she was "really going to miss her," but "thank you for holding down the fort and showing Bruce the ropes."

> AMANDA: Weird to have such masculine energy in the office!

> AMANDA: Dad is going to be so jealous when he sees a photo of this guy.

> SUSAN: You know I only have eyes for one man on this earth.

> SUSAN: But Bruce is great! I'm so glad to have him on the team. He has that intimidating, brooding voice like Don Draper in Mad Men.

After Susan set up her hotel room, she again drove over to the burger place. She was hungry— aching for it, actually, but she also craved a conversation with that bartender again. She had a hunch he would remember her, as it had only been a few days. When she slipped onto the stool, he snapped his fingers and said, "Hi there! You still want an iced tea?"

"Yes, please," she said. Was he flirting with her? He was definitely at least ten years younger than her. The thought of it thrilled her just the slightest bit.

"And a bacon cheeseburger?"

"I think I'll go with a veggie burger today," Susan replied with a grin.

"Heart health. I appreciate that," he said. "I should think about that myself."

"You have a few more years of the good stuff before you have to worry, I think," Susan said.

It was still before the dinner rush and still a few hours before the real sports began. Yet again, the bartender clicked through and found the news, which discussed the opening statements of the Marcie Shean trial. Thankfully, it seemed the part with Susan's speech had already been shown, and they now focused on the prosecution.

"Phew," the bartender said as he placed the glass of iced tea before her. "Can't get it out of my head sometimes, you know? That he worked here. That he had this whole life here. And then one day got involved with the wrong people."

"Awful," Susan breathed.

"I mean, I've been to that house before," the guy continued. He seemed to say it as though he thought it would impress Susan.

"What house?"

"It was kind of like their meeting point, I think, where they passed out the drugs and gave them to the other dealers. I normally don't mess with that side of things, but I had this girlfriend once who was friends with one of the top guys. They had gone to kindergarten and everything together, and she said that he was a really good guy, deep-down, even though he had done some pretty not-so-good stuff."

Susan arched an eyebrow. "Like murder, perhaps?"

The guy shrugged. "I know it sounds crazy. The guy was nice to me, but I was Jan's boyfriend, you know, so he had to be."

"What was this guy's name?"

"Jimmy," the guy told her. "He actually came from money, I guess, but his parents kicked him out and he fell on hard times and then boom. He's the guy involved in all this stuff."

Susan sipped her beer. "So I guess things didn't work out with Jan?"

"Naw, man. She ran off with one of the line cooks from this very restaurant," the bartender said with a sarcastic smile. "I have bad luck. Real bad luck. I guess my luck isn't as bad as old Freddy's, but close."

"Where exactly is this house?" Susan asked.

She half-expected the bartender to step back and accuse her of something. But he seemed so open, so trusting.

"It's in Southie, just around the corner from where Freddy and Marcie lived together," he said. "You can't miss it. I mean, it just feels like a drug house outside, you know?"

Susan had grown up on cozy Martha's Vineyard, but upon her arrival to Newark and after her fall into the world of criminal law, she'd seen her fair share of drug houses.

"I know what you mean," she told him. "It's all fascinating how close you are to this trial."

"Too close," the bartender said. "But like I said. I just

think about Marcie sometimes. She must be terrified. I don't know how they managed to frame her for something like this. But just look at that sweet face. She never did drugs a day in her life."

Susan wasn't so sure about that, either. She had seen plenty of sweet-faced women over the years who were big into drugs.

But he was right. Marcie seemed different than them, somehow.

Susan ate her veggie burger and drank one-half of her iced tea. She then left a thirty-five percent tip and bid the bartender goodbye.

"Hope you'll be back soon?" he said as she stepped back toward the door.

"It's my new favorite place," she told him.

In a sense, her current rush toward Boston really reminded her of her long-ago run to Newark. Everything in her life back on the Vineyard seemed suddenly unstable; Scott had stepped back a bit, and the future was now in flux. She had to be powerful in ways she couldn't fully understand. As she drove toward Southie, she thanked the stars above that she wasn't nineteen any longer. At least now, she had her own wisdom to lean on.

The house around the corner from where Freddy and Marcie had once lived and loved did, in fact, feel like a "drug house." Susan stopped the engine about a block away and rifled through her glove box for pepper spray, which she tucked into the very top layer of her purse for easy access. When she placed her heel on the pavement outside of her car, her heart screamed with anxiety, but she lifted her chin. The witnesses she'd collected weren't enough. She needed something more. And maybe this guy Jimmy had some kind of clue.

Three men stood outside of the house smoking cigarettes and chatting in that way men like that did— as though everything they said was meant to make the others jealous. Susan slowed her walk as she approached so that the man in the midst of his story yanked his head around.

"Hey, pretty mama," he said.

It had been a really long time since Susan had been cat-called. She forced herself not to think about it. Instead, she brightened her face and said, "Good evening. How are you guys doing?"

"Not too shabby," another of them said. He blinked at her with distrust and sucked at a cigarette until the tip of it burned bright orange.

Susan's eyes turned toward the house. It flashed with light from the television.

"Can we help you with something?" one of the guys asked.

"Actually, yes," Susan said. "I'd like to speak with Jimmy, if possible."

The three of them turned their heads inward. The guy on the right shrugged and muttered, "She doesn't look like a cop."

Another of them said, "She could be like, a relative or something."

"I don't mean him any harm at all," Susan said suddenly. "I just want to ask him about a mutual friend we have. I need his help."

The man in the middle asked her to follow him up the steps. Once up there, he said, "Stay here on this stoop, okay?" It seemed like they didn't want her to enter and that was fine with her. The place terrified her to the bone.

Susan waited outside. The other two stomped up the

stairs and then asked her if she wanted a cigarette. She thanked them but declined, although she was almost jittery enough to accept, just to do something with her hands. A few minutes later, a man of about thirty-five came outside. He puffed on what looked like a joint, and he looked at her with glossed-over eyes.

"I've never seen you before in my life," he said.

"Hi. My name is Susan," she said. "You must be Jimmy."

"Who told you to find me here?"

Susan gave a half-shrug. "Friends of mine."

"That sounds pretty weird. What do you want here? You want me to sell to you or something?"

Susan hoped that her plan of attack was appropriate. She remembered the pepper spray; she had it right beneath her hand.

"I'm actually the lawyer representing Marcie George, the young woman whose boyfriend was murdered not far from here," she explained.

Jimmy's eyes widened the slightest bit. "You're repping Marcie, huh?"

Susan nodded. Her heart quickened.

"Well, that's too bad what happened to Freddy. But he honestly had it coming," Jimmy said finally.

Susan arched an eyebrow. "What do you mean?"

"I guess since you found me here, you know that Freddy was involved in some bad stuff. He owed me a lot of money— no two ways about it. I'm not the murdering type, but others around here, well. I'm sure they didn't go there to kill him. Maybe just scare him? Who knows. But they're good at what they do. And they somehow pinned it on Marcie. I know Marcie and Freddy had their problems, but she loved that man to pieces. She loved him

A Vineyard Wedding

more than he deserved to be loved. And I don't think she cares just what happens to her now. She looks so defeated when I see her on TV."

Susan's heart swelled. "I have to get her out of this, Jimmy. She doesn't deserve life in prison. And she's so young. She deserves to find space and time to heal. She deserves to build a new life."

Jimmy furrowed his brow. "I guess you're struggling, building a case."

"I kind of fell into this at the last minute. But I'd like to ask you if you'd consider testifying with what you know," Susan said.

"On the witness stand? Like on TV?" He looked doubtful.

"It really could save Marcie forever," Susan said. "And I wouldn't ask you any questions that led anyone to build a case against you. You wouldn't be in any trouble. Please. Maybe you don't know who actually killed him, but you can build a reasonable doubt that Marcie wasn't the one who did it."

Jimmy turned to watch as a dark car eased down the block a bit too slowly. Susan's ears screamed with fear.

Finally, he nodded. He stabbed his hand in his pocket, seemingly exasperated, and said, "Okay, Susan. Let me give you my number. We'll make this work."

Susan could hardly believe it. "Thank you. Thank you so much."

"Let's get Marcie back out in the world," Jimmy said. "She deserves to see the sun again.

Chapter Fourteen

The prosecution pulled out several witnesses the following day— neighbors who had heard Marcie and Freddy fighting, friends who had seen Marcie once throw a glass of wine at Freddy's head, and of course, all of Freddy's family, who pointed to Marcie as the "devil" who'd broken up their family and turned Freddy into this bad person. Susan did her best to cross-examine every witness, asking if they had ever grown angry with their partners or had little arguments that had resulted in bigger outcomes. Obviously, every one of them had to say yes. Still, one of the final witnesses of the day did put a wrench in things. Apparently, once Marcie had had a bout of road rage and actually purposefully ran her car into another man's fender. Susan turned her eyes toward Marcie's face, which told a story of regret and shame.

"What happened there?" Susan asked Marcie after the session had concluded for the day.

Marcie shrugged. "I had just been fighting with Freddy. I'd threatened to leave him, and he hadn't acted like that was a big deal at all. I lost my mind. I would have done something like that to anyone who got in my way. I felt crazy, like I was going to lose my mind."

Susan buzzed her lips. She lifted her watch to check the time and noted that she still had enough of it to head back to the Vineyard to meet her family for a festival that was happening in Oak Bluffs. She and Marcie had had a longer meeting earlier that day, during which Susan had told her about Jimmy and the potential of these other dealers, who'd probably had something to do with Freddy's murder. Marcie's reaction had been strained, hardly visible. Susan had wondered if this meant that she had barked up the wrong tree. Still, Jimmy was the only leg on which the case stood. He had to come through in some way.

Susan arrived back at Oak Bluffs around seven in the evening, just as the festival flourished with bustling crowds and live music and vibrant clowns and full sails from approaching boats. Susan parked her car off to the side, near the Sunrise Cove itself, and stepped out just as Lola and Tommy walked off of Tommy's boat on the nearby docks. Tommy's arm wrapped firmly around Lola's waist as they walked, and Lola tenderly lifted her chin to dot a kiss on his lips. Susan's heart surged with love for them. All those years, she had thought her baby sister, Lola, would never find lasting happiness with the perfect guy. But she had.

Susan headed toward the crowd. She wasn't quick enough to catch Tommy and Lola, but she soon ran into several people she knew well, including her best friends from high school, Lily and Sarah, who she hadn't caught up with in quite some time.

"Where the heck have you been!" Lily cried as she

wrapped her in a hug. "Sarah and I were just saying that we felt like we lost you again."

"I've been so swamped with this case. I just got back from Boston, in fact. I'm trying to do too much at once."

"As usual," Sarah affirmed. "Have a glass of wine with us! We insist."

Susan scrunched her nose and scanned the crowd. In truth, she wanted to find Amanda and debrief her about what had happened at the trial that day. As it stood, however, she couldn't avoid her dear friends forever.

They waited in line near the music tent for a glass of wine. Zach Walters stood center-stage with his guitar and crooned out. His blue eyes were iridescent, even from fifty feet back. Susan drew a line from his eyes, all the way through the crowd, where she discovered Christine and Amanda together. Susan reasoned that Audrey had had to stay home with the baby.

Lily and Sarah tried their best to keep Susan for longer than a single glass. But mid-way through their sip and catch-up, none other than Scott and Kellan marched directly past their table. Susan's heart leaped into her throat. Since their heart-to-heart chat by the water, she hadn't seen nor heard much from Scott. She had suspected they both had a lot to think about.

Now, though, as their eyes met, Susan felt suddenly overwhelmed by it all. She nearly toppled the table over as she stood to greet him. It was as though her body had craved him, especially after all the fearful and dangerous things she had done in Boston.

"Kellan! Scott!"

"There she goes. Our little runaway," Lily quipped as she clucked her tongue.

"I'll explain later. But I really have to go," Susan said

as she lifted her wine to cheer them. "It's been a complicated time for me. But I love you two forever, and it was so nice seeing your beautiful faces. You know that."

"We know," they said in sing-song voices.

Susan stepped easily toward Kellan and Scott, who were in the midst of a vibrant conversation about a sports team. Scott beamed at her as Kellan illustrated his point with a fist slammed against his opposite palm.

"Things are getting pretty heated around here," he explained to Susan.

"I can see that."

Kellan drew himself around, surprised to see her. "Oh. Hi, Susan. Good to see you."

Susan was surprised not to hear any hint of jealousy, anger, or annoyance in his voice. A step in the right direction, she supposed.

"Hi, Kellan! What do you think of our festival here in Oak Bluffs?"

"It's really nice, actually. I just won this stuffed animal at the game over there." Kellan drew himself further around to show a stuffed duck beneath his arm.

Susan laughed and said she was impressed. "I don't think I've ever won anything here. I've lost a lot of my dignity, though. That's for sure."

Scott placed a hand on her lower back even as she and Kellan continued to talk. This pleased he, as she felt it proved to Kellan that she and Scott were together, whether he liked it or not. Scott even offered to grab them both second drinks, including a Coke for Kellan. This left Kellan and Susan in conversation, which seemed to flow naturally.

"How has it been at school these days?" Susan asked. "I guess the year ends pretty soon?"

"Yeah. It took a bit of adjusting. And I guess I won't really get over that for a while," Kellan explained. "But generally, the people here on the island are friendlier than they are back in Boston. I have to take my wins where I can."

"That's all we can do in this life," Susan said. "And you know, me and your dad met at that high school, if you can believe it."

"He told me. I mean, he wouldn't shut up about it last year," Kellan told her. "He'd asked me years ago if I ever wanted to come live with him here on the island. He said it was the perfect place to grow up. But I was always resistant. Maybe I was a momma's boy for a while. I don't know." Kellan shrugged.

"No harm in loving your mom," Susan replied.

Kellan gave her a somber smile. "I guess not."

"And you're still so new here. I think your dad's right. This is a wonderful place to grow up. You'll find your footing, eventually. And we'll help you if you'll let us."

Scott arrived back with the drinks, and the conversation flowed elsewhere. But throughout, Kellan frequently met Susan's gaze and asked decent questions. He seemed to find some kind of grove after so much bad footing. When he went off to the bathroom about an hour later, Susan lifted her eyes to Scott's and said, "What kind of witchcraft did you do to make Kellan act so much... better toward me?"

Scott laughed. He then turned his eyes out toward the horizon as though he wanted to gather his thoughts. "To be honest, Susan, he's noticed how down I've been since the other night. He finally got it out of me— that we weren't sure about the wedding. That things are up in the air because of him. He took a really long walk down the beach. I was afraid he would never come back. But when he returned, he just said, 'I want to make this work, and I don't want to be the cause of anything bad happening.' And he's tried to change a lot since then. We still have tiffs, of course. And I know it'll take time. But I think we're headed somewhere, and he's really making an effort to change. And we want you within our lives, forever. That said, I don't know fully about this June 19th date yet."

"I understand."

"But I do know that we have to decide soon. Sooner than soon."

"Yes. Preferably, sooner than soon," Susan affirmed with a smile. Her heart felt squeezed at the idea of calling it off the day before. The island would say— like daughter, like mother, and all in the same year!

"Tell me. How did it go in Boston today?" Scott asked. His eyes sparkled with intrigue.

"It went well, I think. I'm moving in a good direction. It's been complicated and emotional. But then again, everything in this business is like that," Susan said.

"You amaze me. Every single day," Scott said. He then dropped down and kissed her softly, tenderly. "And I'm going to spend the rest of my life with you. Lucky for me, the rest of my life started all those years ago. And I never really let you go."

Chapter Fifteen

The following afternoon, the ever-organized, ever-stellar Amanda was so nervous during the beginning of the trial that she tore at the edge of her pad of paper, making little scraps of yellow fall to the floor. Susan grabbed her wrist and nodded to the wreckage, and Amanda's eyes widened humorously. "Oh! I didn't even notice," she said.

"It's okay," Susan breathed. "I feel a bit outside my element, too."

At that moment, the guards led Marcie Shean into the court. She slid onto the wooden bench alongside Susan and dropped her chin in greeting. She seemed somehow sallower; the bones on the upper part of her spine popped up even more on her neck, and her fingers were mere bones, splayed out across her knees. Behind them, Mr. Shean spoke in hushed, angry tones to the younger brother. Susan wasn't sure why the younger brother wasn't in school, as there were still a few weeks left of school before summer break. Probably, Mr. Shean didn't have anyone to ask to look out for the boy. Or, she supposed, if these were the last moments the brother would see Marcie out of prison, perhaps he wanted to count them up.

But these were heinous thoughts. She had to remain positive and clear-headed.

And it was finally her turn to call her witness from the drug house— Jimmy.

Jimmy sat fidgeting in the witness chair. His "I swear to tell the whole truth and nothing but the truth" oath was said with sloppy syllables, and when Susan got a tiny bit too close to him, she caught a horrible whiff of cigarette smoke and something else— maybe dirty laundry. Still, it was clear he very much represented a world Freddy Peterson was a part of. Jimmy would paint that picture for the jury.

"Hello, Jimmy. Thanks for being here today."

"Hi." His shirt looked uncomfortable on him. He tugged at the collar and glanced toward the clock.

"I wonder if you could describe to the court a bit about your relationship with Freddy Peterson, the man who was murdered on November 13th."

Jimmy cleared his throat. "I knew Freddy for years. Guess I met him about five years ago. He worked at that restaurant, the expensive one he met Marcie at. Was a good guy."

"Were you good friends with Freddy Peterson?"

"I wouldn't say that, no," Jimmy replied. "Although we ended up living close to one another, so I saw him around quite a bit. And he stopped by my place a lot."

"Why did he stop by your place?"

Jimmy's eyes glittered. "Well, he and I tended to like the same pastime, if you know what I mean. Something to kick back. Unwind."

"I see. But you still wouldn't have called him your friend?"

"Naw. More of an acquaintance."

"Do you know the other kinds of people Freddy Peterson was hanging around with?"

Jimmy grimaced again. He genuinely looked in pain.

"Freddy didn't have many friends besides Marcie. I know he loved her a lot, even though he complained about her all the time. That's just what guys do, you know? We take what we can from the women we love, and then we complain about it."

This time, when he smiled, he showed a gold tooth off to the left side of his mouth.

"But anyway, he wanted to make some extra cash, and he got to talking to another buddy of mine, who could hook him up with another guy— a big dealer in the area. At least, that's what some say. I'm not really into anything hard, you know?"

"I see. So you suspect that Freddy was dealing drugs?"

"I don't suspect it. I know it for a fact, ma'am. And the higher-ups he was dealing with weren't exactly on the nicer side. And Freddy, like I said, he was strapped for cash. I heard even as early as last summer that Freddy wasn't really making the appropriate payments to the higher-ups. Still, he and Marcie seemed just about broke at all times."

Susan furrowed her brow. "Where do you think the money was going, if not to these higher-ups and not back to their lifestyle?"

Jimmy shrugged. "It's always the same, isn't it? He was using. I saw him on the street, maybe in late October, and he was skinny as a palm tree. He could hardly keep himself upright. If someone else didn't kill him, he was well on his way."

There was a gasp from Freddy's mother. Several people in the court turned heads and whispered to one another frantically. The judge pounded his gavel against the wood and hollered for silence, and slowly everyone calmed down again. But clearly, Jimmy had caused a fuss.

"Is it reasonable to assume that one of these people involved in this drug world killed Freddy and not Marcie?" Susan asked, point-blank.

Jimmy nodded. "Definitely. Much more likely than Marcie doing it. Marcie and Freddy had their problems, but they would have never turned on each other like that." He gave a final nod off in Marcie's direction, but Marcie didn't lift her eyes to see it.

Susan had, of course, told Marcie about the Jimmy situation. She'd also informed Marcie that she planned to have Marcie on the stand next. Still, once Marcie sat in the very chair Jimmy had just left and after a lackluster cross-examination from the prosecutor, she looked squeamish and strange. If Susan hadn't known better, she might have suspected the girl was guilty. This sort of look backtracked on the good that Jimmy had just done. Inwardly, Susan cursed.

"Marcie. I want to ask you today about Freddy's drug use. It's been suggested that he was using pretty heavily during his final days."

Marcie's chin began to quiver. Her hands then shot over her cheeks as a sob escaped her throat. Again, the courtroom muttered with surprise.

"He was so messed up," Marcie cried out. "So messed up, I can't even— it's so hard to talk about."

Susan's heart dropped. This wasn't how she had

expected Marcie to answer; in fact, they'd rehearsed it far differently.

"He just changed so much. His personality was all over the place. He was often violent. He threw things! He once threw a lamp across the room! I was like, how do you think we're going to pay to buy a new lamp? And he just laughed in my face. It was awful." Marcie continued to weep.

Susan allowed the girl a moment to cry. She then stepped forward, dropped her chin, and said, "Marcie. I know this is painful for you. I understand your boyfriend was violent due to drug use. But tell us here, now. Did you kill Freddy Peterson on that day in November?"

Marcie shook her head wildly so that her blond hair uncoiled from its up-do. "No. I didn't kill him. I couldn't have."

At least there, she sounded somewhat resolute.

But when the prosecutor, Paul Soloman, stood for cross-examination, Susan watched as Marcie melted in the palm of his hand.

"Marcie. We learned a great deal today about your boyfriend's temperament," Paul said. "Tell us. What did you do all those times that he became violent? Did you just stand there and take it?"

Again, Marcie's chin began to quiver. She started to answer, but Paul cut her off.

"Did you just let him rip into you? Did you think, even once, to call someone for help?"

"I didn't know what to do. I knew he was messed up on drugs, and I—"

"But what made you stay with him? Isn't it possible that you stayed until your breaking point? Isn't it possible that you told yourself, always, 'I'll stay one more day,' or,

'He'll change. He'll change!' and then one day, he came after you while you held a knife, and—"

"NO!" Marcie wailed the word.

But Susan could sense it in the eyes of the jury. Paul had painted a near-perfect picture. And perhaps Susan's strategy had backfired. Susan leaped up from the wooden bench and cried, "Objection!"

And the judge sustained it.

But the damage had already been done.

Chapter Sixteen

Susan placed her suit jacket into her suitcase and muttered to herself angrily. When she walked across the hotel room, her heels clacked a little too loudly. She yanked her curling iron out of the power outlet with such force that Amanda whistled. "Mom, you gotta calm down. Today wasn't as bad as you think it was."

"I just hate the way he picked her apart," Susan snarled. She took to the zipper on her suitcase as though it, too, were an enemy. "I just feel she came off a bit whiny today. A bit like she's guilty. I don't know. I could sense it in the air. Couldn't you?"

Amanda grimaced. "It isn't over. There's still time for more witness testimony from Jimmy. And maybe Jimmy can lead us to another option. Besides, he did create reasonable doubt—"

"Sure, but I think that reasonable doubt died on the hardwood floor," Susan replied. She placed her hands on her waist and blinked out the window into the late-May

A Vineyard Wedding

sunshine. "Maybe I shouldn't leave Boston yet. I should stick around here."

"Mom. Don't you remember? We have plans this afternoon," Amanda reminded her. "And you promised me you would take a small break from the case."

Susan furrowed her brow. "Okay. I kind of remember that."

Amanda jumped up and laced her arms around her mother from behind. "Don't you remember? You made a promise to that other child of yours. Tall? Handsome? Name starts with a J?"

Susan's heart warmed the slightest bit. "He must think I'm a monster of a mother. I don't think I've called him in over two weeks?"

"Naw. He has enough on his plate with Kristen's pregnancy," Amanda said. "And the twins! Gosh, they must be even bigger than the last time we saw them. Remember last year? How they howled non-stop, no matter what?"

"Yeah. I'm sure by now that they're reciting Shakespeare and holding intellectual discussions about astrophysics," Susan said with a funny grin.

The drive from Boston to Newark took a little less than four hours. It was a warm morning, and Susan drew the driver's side window open the slightest bit and eased her fingers over the glass. Beside her, Amanda hovered over a law textbook; she'd decided to take a heavy online summer course load, with the potential to return to Rutgers in person in the fall. She hadn't yet decided, she'd said, but beyond anything, they both knew that Amanda would ultimately return to the Sheridan Law Office once she had passed her bar and practice alongside Susan and their new attorney, Bruce.

"And your father is really going to come for lunch?" Susan asked after nearly an entire hour of silence.

Amanda lifted her chin. "Yes. He said he would. Is that okay for you?"

"Of course." Susan cleared her throat and then added, "Maybe it's weird to say to you since you're his daughter, but I hardly remember my feelings for Richard. It feels like a thing that happened to some other person, in some other life."

Amanda shrugged. "It doesn't affect me to hear that. Jake and I always knew you guys weren't so well-matched. Great in the courtroom, though— an unstoppable force."

Susan chuckled. "That's right, we were. No better team on the east coast. I'll never forget."

* * *

Susan pulled up into the once-familiar driveway of her son's large four-bedroom house, located not far from the home where she'd raised her babies with Richard. Around a year before, just before she had headed to the Vineyard for a "surprise visit," she'd planned to reside for a while at this very home. "Can you believe I actually offered to care for the twins, Jake and Kristen?" Susan said as she gathered up supplies from the back of her car, including two bottles of chilled wine from the nearby grocery store and a big thing of potato salad.

"You would have gone nuts," Amanda agreed.

Just before they got to the front door, Jake flung it open. He had one of the twins— his daughter, Samantha, straddled at his side, and it looked like he had a bit of toothpaste in his hair. He was every bit Richard Harris from some twenty years ago, but with that typical Jake smile.

"Jake!" Susan cried as she flung her arms around both him and his daughter. "Look at the two of you! And oh my goodness, it already smells so good in there."

"Kristen decided to try a new recipe," Jake said with a grimace. "So we'll see if it turns out."

"I heard that!" Kristen called from the kitchen. After a moment, she, too, appeared. Her pregnant belly bulged beneath her light pink spring dress, and her right hand led the sheepish-looking other twin, Cody.

Susan stepped forward, knelt down, and in a flash, Cody rushed for her. Susan had been petrified that her grandchildren had forgotten her, as she had been gone during this formative year. But Cody squealed, "Grandma!" directly into her ear, proof that they'd not forgotten, and they hadn't gotten any quieter, either.

"We set up a big table in the sun outside," Kristen said as she dropped a kiss on Susan's cheek. "Go out and make yourselves comfortable. Richard and Penelope will be here shortly. Apparently, Richard wanted to stop at some new natural wine store. You know how he and Pen are. Always hip with the trends."

Susan laughed inwardly as she joined Amanda, Jake, Cody, and Samantha outside at a large glass table. It felt strangely outside of time, this reunion. She tried to imagine explaining it to a previous version of herself. *"Listen up, Susie; you and Rich won't make it. And someday soon, you'll be engaged to Scott and meet with Richard and that little secretary of yours, who is pregnant with his baby. The weirdest part? You'll be absolutely fine with it."*

Richard appeared out back a few minutes later. He

lifted the natural wine in greeting as his eyes met with Susan's. They glittered with recognition as he said, "Susan. It's so good to see you. I couldn't help but notice that case of yours. I've been following it closely. It seems like a real doozy."

Susan stood and gave Richard a half-hug. Penelope appeared behind him in an iconic dark blue dress, with a large slit up the left leg. Her pregnant belly was fit for a pregnancy magazine, and she held it tenderly as she gave Susan a strangely jealous look. Obviously, Richard had tried to discuss the case with Penelope, who probably hadn't understood a lot of the intricacies.

Not that it mattered at all.

"It's been a real trip," Susan affirmed. "I was asked last minute to take the case on. Actually, trip isn't the right word. Nightmare is more like it."

"But you know how Mom loves a good puzzle to solve," Amanda said as she uncorked the wine bottle and began to pour helpings all around.

Kristen served lemon chicken and a light pasta salad, along with freshly-baked bread and slabs of various fine cheese from a nearby dairy farm. She sat, exhausted, next to Jake as Cody and Samantha ran rampant around the yard.

"Do you think they want to eat?" Amanda asked.

"It's just better to let them tire themselves out when they feel like running," Kristen said. "We're basically slaves to their every whim."

"Can't wait for parenthood," Penelope said with a vibrant laugh.

If Susan wasn't mistaken, Richard turned the slightest shade of green at that. But in a flash, he grabbed Penelope's hand and lifted it to his lips to kiss it. Obviously, he was leaning in. He had to.

"And how is that idiot ex of yours, Amanda?" Richard asked mid-way through the dinner. His voice was loud, domineering, and Susan resented it.

Amanda just shrugged, though. "He's halfway around the world like he's been since he left me at the altar."

Penelope pursed her lips nervously. "The way you say it. Like you don't care at all!"

"It was for the best. Look." Amanda leafed her phone from her purse and began to flash images up for all to see. "Look. He went skydiving and learned to scuba dive and caught this enormous fish outside of Tokyo and well, he's done a whole lot more living in the past few months than I ever dreamed of doing. I say good for him."

"Healthy," Penelope affirmed as she plopped an olive on her tongue. "And I don't suppose you have anyone else lined up?"

Amanda's cheeks flushed pink. Penelope snapped her fingers and said, "She does! Oh, you do. Tell us everything."

Susan knew it was her turn to save the day. She flashed her eyes toward Richard and said, "I guess you probably haven't heard that my sister, Christine, is pregnant, too?"

Richard almost spit his drink out but then said. "I thought she couldn't get pregnant?"

"That's apparently what the doctors told her, but it happened."

"I guess there's something in the air," Richard replied. "Sure is."

Richard chewed contemplatively. "And you're getting married in about three weeks. Aren't you?"

Susan hadn't given true thought to the wedding since she'd last seen Scott. The entire concept terrified her. "Seems like it," was what she chose to say, which was enough to get her off the hook.

"Jake, I meant to tell you," Richard said suddenly. "They have an opening for you at the country club."

"No way!" Jake's eyes actually lit up. "Golf Sunday?"

"You bet," Richard said. "Now that we're both going to be young dads together..."

"We'll have to stay sane together."

"Don't worry, Penelope," Kristen said mischievously. "We can have our wine afternoons while the boys run all over that green. That is, of course, after the babies comes."

"I thought you'd never say so," Penelope said. "Gosh, I know it's typical, but being a new mom is one of the most terrifying things! I've already started looking at preschools. I think it's really important to have all this prepared, even before they're bigger than a pinecone."

Kristen laughed. "Don't I know it! Especially here in Newark. Things get competitive and fast."

Susan and Amanda exchanged glances. It seemed clear that this was no longer their world. Susan leaned back in her chair and sipped her wine, with its dense texture and musky aftertaste, and allowed the strange sadness to fold over her. It was remarkable that she and Amanda had built this whole other life. But these people — so many of them, she loved with her whole heart. And she knew, in her leaving, she had left a piece of her soul here. One she might never fully get back. Already, Richard and Jake were best friends; Penelope and Kristen were chummy, and the grandkids would grow bigger and more boisterous by the day. Susan would do her best to keep her link, but by the day, it grew weaker. It was just the nature of things and time.

Chapter Seventeen

That evening, Lola and Christine sat at the back picnic table at the Sheridan house, both with their arms crossed over their chests. Their faces were stoic, and their body position was reminiscent of Marcie Shean on the witness stand. Susan stood before them with a glass of wine in hand as they peppered her with questions.

"We have to tell Charlotte what's up with the wedding," Christine said. "Do you and Scott know one way or the other yet?"

"Because Charlotte said we could still get some of the deposit back if we pull out now. But by next week? No way," Lola affirmed.

"Have you really been telling Charlotte about all my dirty laundry?" Susan asked. She shifted her weight as exhaustion settled over her.

"Come on. She's family!" Lola replied.

"Yeah, but she's not us," Susan replied.

"We didn't tell her everything. Just that it's been complicated with Scott's son coming to town."

"Everyone knows that Scott Frampton worships the ground you walk on," Lola said. "It's just not fair to anyone— not to you or Scott or the wedding venue or any of the guests, to keep this decision hovering. I know it's making you sick."

"That's not really why I'm sick," Susan protested.

"We know. We know. The trial is getting to you." Christine glowered as she sipped her sparkling water. "But come on. You were supposed to be hyper-focused on building this life with Scott. And now, it's like everything is on the back burner? And you look sick, Susan. Like, your cheeks are hollow, and it's like you're not eating enough, and..."

Susan dropped down to the other side of the picnic table, placed her glass of wine on the wood, and held her face in her hands.

"Just call him. Ask him point-blank what he's thinking," Lola urged. "That way, we can make a new date. Maybe even something in late September or early October? After the tourist season, maybe?"

"It would definitely remove the stress from you both," Christine said.

"Since when are you the practical one here?" Susan asked sharply.

Christine and Lola exchanged pointed looks.

"Jeez. Sorry," Christine offered flippantly. "We just want to help in any way we can. And we see that you're—"

"Falling apart a bit. I know," Susan finished her sentence.

There was the buzzing of a motor. Susan glanced down toward the beach, where Sam, Amanda, Audrey, and Noah appeared in the speedboat. They looked so vibrant, so excited. Amanda and Audrey's hair flowed wildly through the breeze, and their legs already flashed brown with late-spring tans. They were portraits of youth and vitality. Susan's heart ached with fatigue. It was such a contrast.

As they latched up the boat, Sam lifted his phone to his ear. Susan could see it all the way from the porch: there was something wrong. He hustled up the hill toward the house and hollered to Susan.

"Hey! Susan! There's an incident at the Sunrise Cove. We need to get over there right now. It's just Natalie at the desk."

Susan's heart leaped into her throat. "What kind of incident?" she cried. She rushed through the shadows of the house, past the sleeping Max in his little carrier, and all the way to the driveway, where she leaped into the passenger seat of Sam's car. It was all a mad dash. There wasn't a moment of clarity. Sam pressed his foot on the gas as Susan demanded more information. "Did Natalie say anything else?"

"She's apparently hiding in the office. Zach called the police from the bistro."

Susan splayed her hands on the dash as they rushed toward the Inn. Once there, they hopped from the car and ran headlong for the foyer door. They then peered through the window as a number of sirens blared behind them.

There, Susan recognized Scott. He had a man pressed against the top of the front desk, with both of his hands latched behind his back. Scott's muscles were tense; he clearly used all his power as the man beneath him flailed around, attempting to flee.

A Vineyard Wedding

Susan crashed through the door, gasping for air. "Scott?" she cried.

Scott turned his head wildly toward her. His eyes flashed. "Susan. You shouldn't have come."

"Is that her? Is that that f—" But before the man beneath Scott could blare out his curse words, Scott pressed harder on his wrists so that he howled with pain.

In a moment, the police burst through the foyer door. They latched the man's wrists together with handcuffs and lifted him to standing. The man was maybe thirty or thirty-five, clearly strung-out, with beady black eyes and light skin tinged with red. When he spoke, his accent was hard, clearly from the city of Boston. He glared at Susan with malice.

"Susan Sheridan," the man growled.

At this moment, the police officer yanked him toward the door. Susan stepped to the side. All the while, she kept her eyes latched to his.

"Susan Sheridan, why don't you just stay on your cozy little island and keep to yourself?" the man continued. He leered at her ominously, then; Susan felt she'd never seen a more horrendous smile.

Susan was speechless. She knew there was nothing she could say, not there in front of the police. Not with Scott beside her.

Suddenly, the man hacked up a huge spit and blasted it across the floor at her feet. Susan kept her face stoic. She knew better than to show such a man any sign of weakness.

In a moment, the officer pushed the man into the back of the police car. Another office remained at the inn to interview witnesses. He stepped toward Zach first, as Zach had been the first to dial 9-1-1.

At this first moment of reprieve, Susan spun into Scott's arms and allowed him to hold her tight in his arms. Her legs shook so bad that her knees knocked together. Fear rushed through her. It seemed clear that whoever that man was, he was associated with the case, and he hadn't come to Martha's Vineyard for any reason beyond causing potential harm to Susan herself.

Scott leaned back and splayed a hand across her cheek. He shook his head slowly, softly, and placed his nose on hers. "Susan. What the heck have you gotten yourself involved in?"

Susan allowed herself to laugh the slightest bit. "It's been a really wild time."

Scott's hand wrapped around the back of her head. "I am so glad I was here. One of the cabinets upstairs had broken, and Natalie asked me to take a look at it."

"You saved the day all over again," Susan said. She then turned toward the back hallway, where a flustered Natalie appeared. Her cheeks were stained with tears.

Zach finished up his conversation with the cop. The cop then took Scott's statement. Slowly, the air in the foyer returned to normal. Sam bustled behind the front desk to discuss what had happened with worried guests. He still wore his swim trunks and a light blue polo shirt, but he exuded professionalism and ensured all the guests were taken care of.

The cop stopped at Susan just before he left. "I have a feeling we'll need to take you down to the station for more information. We're going to speak with the guy first. Why don't you relax for the night. You'll hear from us tomorrow."

"Sounds good," Susan said. Her voice wavered the slightest bit.

When the cop disappeared, Scott wrapped a hand around Susan's waist and said, "I have to go pick Kellan up from an after-school activity."

"I'll come with you," Susan told him. The idea of being away from this man— her protector— filled her with dread. She dropped her head on his chest as they walked slowly toward his truck. In the passenger seat, tears rolled down her cheeks.

"Do you have a hunch of who that guy is?" Scott asked as they eased toward the high school.

"I do, actually," Susan whispered. "And if everything works out, he might have just made a huge mistake. He might be the key to my entire case."

Scott shook his head as he drove. "I don't know how you do any of this. It terrifies me."

"It terrifies me, too. But I have to keep fighting. I can't let this guy get to me. Marcie is up in Boston, and she's facing a life sentence. The entire city thinks she's guilty. If that belligerent man just gave himself away..." Susan rubbed her palms together.

"One day at a time," Scott said with a funny laugh. "Let's just focus on tonight. You're safe. For one more day, you're safe."

Chapter Eighteen

When Susan awoke the following morning, she felt the strong arm of Scott Frampton around her stomach, holding her tightly against him. It had been weeks since she had enjoyed such a wonderful feeling— this moment of eternal safety, of comfort, of love, and she allowed herself to stew in the beauty of it, even as Scott's light snores filled the air over them.

The previous night, Scott, Susan, and Kellan had decided to stay at the Sheridan house. There was a comfort in knowing they were all together beneath one roof. Besides, Scott had been the one to add the extra bedrooms downstairs. He had understood that sometimes, the Sheridan family needed to be close, especially after so many years of disconnection.

Kellan hadn't protested the arrangement. In fact, he had immediately suggested that he sleep on the couch. Christine and Lola had both protested and said they insisted he take one of the beds, as they both had elsewhere to stay. Even now, Susan felt she could hear

Kellan's snores rip out from one of the other upstairs bedrooms. The previous night, he'd been so tender with baby Max that her heart had swelled at the sight of it. In truth, Kellan was just a teenaged boy with a huge heart who was on the brink of the turmoil that went with growing up. Susan would be there to help him if he allowed her to.

She knew better than most that you had to be able to trust your guardians to guide you. After her mother's death, she hadn't been able to lean on her father at all. It had caused a near-permanent rift, one they had spent the previous year mending as best as they could. But love was powerful in the Sheridan family; it was almost as though Anna had draped them in it from above.

Christine returned to the house just past seven and announced that she would make everyone a big pancake breakfast. "I've been up since four making scones and croissants at the bistro. Can't say I'm ready to quit yet!" she said as she sifted several cups of flour into a large mixing bowl.

"You're insane, Christine, my queen," Lola said as she poured herself a mug of coffee. "Anyone else? Coffee?"

Kellan lifted his hand, and Lola nodded. "Sure. Cream? Sugar?"

"Black," Kellan affirmed.

Susan and Scott gave one another knowing looks. Sure enough, the moment Kellan sipped his strong black coffee, he grimaced. He didn't say anything, though. He wanted to man up. Be one of the adults.

"Still no word from the station?" Christine asked as she whipped through the pancake batter.

"No," Susan said. "Although I have a hunch they'll call me in this morning."

"Can't believe that guy made it all the way to the Sunrise Cove!" Lola said, her brow furrowed. "I guess it's not so difficult to learn where we're located. All our names are on the website. 'A family inn experience!' Maybe we should change that? Especially if you're going to be working with more criminals?"

Susan shook her head. "I never imagined that merging my old world with my new one would create such a mess. I might have to rethink that after this case."

Christine and Lola exchanged glances again— ones that suggested they'd always suspected this would be an enormous mess.

"All right, I get it. You want to think you're smarter than your big sister," Susan teased. "And maybe, in this very small, very tiny respect, you might be right."

"Finally, I've waited almost forty years to hear that," Lola said with a sigh.

"Oh my gosh! That's right. Lola. The big four-oh this summer," Christine said as she whacked her elbow into Lola's shoulder. "Over the hill!"

"Don't remind me. I'm already a grandmother. What's next?" Lola heaved a sigh.

"How lucky we all are to grow old," Susan said with a wide smile.

"And how lucky the hair-dye manufacturer is to profit off of us," Lola returned.

Susan's phone buzzed on the table. She lifted it and received word that, yes, in fact, the police station needed her to come down in the wake of their interview with the sad sack of a man they'd taken up from the Sunrise Cove the previous evening. Susan's eyes met with Scott's as he nodded.

"Let's take you downtown, Susan Sheridan," he said.

"Sounds so dreary when you say it like that," she returned.

"Kellan? You're good here?"

"All good," Kellan said. He then turned toward Wes, who was stationed in the corner with a newspaper. "Grandpa Wes. I don't suppose you'd like to go out for a little bird watching?"

* * *

Up at the station, one of the officers who had apprehended the subject informed Susan that the man was "incredibly volatile." His name was Marvin. Marvin Stokes.

"He was pretty drunk and high when we picked him up yesterday. And now, he's obviously come down from that, so he's miserable," the cop explained. "He said a lot of jibberish. But he also suggested that you're in some way after him— that you know too much. Anyway, I looked you up, and it seems like you're in the midst of a pretty hefty trial up in Boston. Any chance this has something to do with that?"

"About a one hundred percent chance, yes." Susan arched an eyebrow and then added, "I don't suppose I can talk to him, can I?"

"Of course. We can bring him into the interrogation room for you."

"Perfect."

While the cop arranged for this, Scott gripped Susan's elbow. "Are you sure you want to talk to that raving lunatic?"

"I have to," Susan told him pointedly. "I know I seemed like a frightened little girl last night, but this really means a lot to me. And I have to press him for more info, especially when he's in this kind of state. He's vulnerable right now, and I need to take full advantage of that."

The man who sat across from Susan Sheridan at the interrogation table was sallow; he reeked of urine and sweat, and his shoulders sagged so low that there were big, hollow holes along his neckline. Susan thought of something similar that she had when she'd encountered Jimmy at that drug house. What on earth had happened to this man along the strange and winding road of life? What had led him to this state? Where was his mother? Did anyone love him?

But she couldn't show such compassion. Not now.

Susan pressed RECORD on her phone beneath the table. She then lifted her eyes toward his dead ones and said, "Why did you come to Martha's Vineyard yesterday?"

Martin's eyes rolled back in his head. Susan could practically feel the severity of what he was going through. Guaranteed, it was the start of a withdrawal.

"I came to see you, Susan Sheridan." He licked his lips strangely.

Susan didn't allow herself to react. "Did you come because you're in some way affiliated with Jimmy, who I brought to the witness stand for the case against Marcie Shean?"

"Affiliated? You could say that." Marvin gave her a horrible smile.

"And did you happen to know Freddy Peterson? The man who was murdered on November 13th?"

"Oh, sure. Anyone who was anyone knew Freddy," Marvin returned.

Susan arched an eyebrow. "Can you tell me your history with Freddy Peterson?"

Marvin leaned back. He strained to cross his arms over his chest, although one of his hands remained latched to the table, so he didn't get so far.

"It's difficult to really explain that life to a woman like you. A rich woman, I mean. A woman who grew up with everything."

Susan swallowed the lump in her throat. She was used to these kinds of "insults" from men like him, at least in her previous era of criminal defense.

"Did you kill Freddy Peterson because he owed you money?" Susan asked, point-blank.

At this, Marvin burst into laughter— the kind that showed all three of his bright gold teeth and the depth of his dimples. Susan imagined that he'd actually been quite a cute kid back in the day. She imagined that someone had loved him.

"I didn't kill Freddy."

"But you know who did. And you want to protect them for some reason," Susan shot out, hoping he would take the bait.

Marvin shrugged. "Who's to say? You damn lawyers, on the other side, always make up your own little stories, anyway. Everyone wants to believe that Marcie killed Freddy. It's a romantic idea that the beautiful girl killed her boyfriend. It's perfect for a documentary series, the kind that asks— what made this stunning girl crack?"

Susan's nostrils flared. He had already given her enough to take up to the court in Boston. This idea that the world wanted to believe Marcie had killed Freddy provided such a beautiful, reasonable doubt. Still, she would have loved to press this guy further, to at least produce a name.

"Who introduced you to Freddy, then?" Susan asked.

Marvin clucked his tongue. "You ain't getting that out of me. No way."

"Okay. Well. Maybe they can up in Boston," Susan said. She stood, and her chair squeaked against the cement floor, which made Marvin wince. "I guess I'll see you there soon. Thanks for stopping by the Vineyard when you could. It's particularly beautiful this time of year, isn't it?"

She then sauntered out of the interrogation room and pressed her finger on her phone to stop the recording. Her heart surged into her throat as her eyes found Freddy's. She performed the tiniest of dances there at the police station and said, "I knew she didn't do it. But I'm so, so glad that everywhere I look, there's even more evidence that she's innocent. I'm going to get her out of this. I just know it."

Chapter Nineteen

Susan paced back and forth in the living area at the Sheridan house as she conducted business call after business call with various members of the Boston police force and court system. She'd sent along the recording she had taken, along with what she suspected regarding the actual murderer of Freddy Peterson, and she pressed them to take action and discover the "real story."

"A young, innocent girl is believed to be a murderer in this extremely difficult case, but it seems clear to me that this man's appearance at my family inn is reason enough to prove that there is much more to this case than meets the eye," Susan blared.

When she hung up the phone, she gasped for breath and blinked down at the trail she had dragged back and forth across the rug in the living area. She felt slightly manic, a bit high-strung. When she lifted her eyes to find Scott and Kellan on the back porch, her heart grew tremendously. Their voices merged with the soft rhythm of Wes's, who sat on the other side of the picnic table.

When she joined them, they turned to look at her with bright, vibrant eyes.

"Sorry to interrupt," she said cheerfully.

"Not at all," her father said. "We were just saying how impressed we are with you. Hard to believe you grew up here. From such humble beginnings! Now, you're this high-powered criminal lawyer, and, well..." Wes shook his head. "I know you always were before back in Newark. But this is the first I've really seen you in action. Everyone stops me on the island, completely overwhelmed with the work you've done. I'm so proud of you, honey."

"They stop me, too," Scott chimed in. "I think they think I'm a schlub when compared to you."

"No way," Susan said. She crossed and uncrossed her arms, suddenly embarrassed. She'd been in such a work zone that now, life on the exterior of that seemed strained. "I kind of need to walk or something. Get out of the house."

"I'll join you," Scott said. "Just let me grab something upstairs."

"You guys going to be okay here?" Susan asked.

"Kellan is an amazing bird scout," Wes said. "I know we discussed it last summer, but he's really put it to action today. We might go out later if my old legs don't give out on me."

"We get a pretty good view of some of them from right here on this porch," Kellan said. "And now that it's nearly summer, we'll have a cornucopia of varied creatures. So much better than in Boston. There, the pickings were slim."

"I can imagine," Wes affirmed. "Didn't I always tell you, Susie? The city was bunk."

A Vineyard Wedding

"You always did say that, Dad," Susan replied with a laugh.

"We'll make Kellan an islander yet," Wes said.

* * *

Scott appeared downstairs with a backpack. Susan slipped on her tennis shoes and muttered mostly to herself about the case until she and Scott slipped out the back door. Scott's fingers found hers as they walked along, heading toward the line of trees off to the northeast side of the house.

"Gosh, it's nice to just walk with you," Susan said evenly.

"It was always my favorite thing— to walk with you even when we don't have any direction in mind."

"Like now?"

Scott tilted his head and gave her a mischievous smile. "Actually, I have a destination for us. If you don't protest."

She tilted her head to get a better look at his face. "Why would I?"

"It's a bit— strange." Scott's grip on her fingers grew stronger, more insistent. They continued through the woods and then walked down lower toward the waterline. Susan knew that they'd walked away from the Sheridan property line but that nobody had lived down in this area of the woods for at least two decades, maybe more.

The house that came into view both surprised her and reminded her of a long-ago dream-like memory. In that memory, the house, which had belonged to the Jacobsons, had been regal, made of stone, almost like a miniature castle there by the sands. In the wake of the Jacobson's departure, the house had turned toward ruin, and for whatever reason, nobody had scooped it up in all the years since.

But as they stood on the hill overlooking the house, Susan breathed, "It looks like someone has restored the entire house."

Scott's thumb traced the top of her hand delicately. After a long, pregnant pause, he said, "We don't have to live here if you don't want."

Susan's jaw dropped. She flung her head round to catch his gaze as he dropped down again on that very hill and positioned himself on one knee.

"It has been one hell of a month for both of us, Susan. But I purchased this house in January with every intention of building it back up in time for our wedding day on June 19th. In the previous weeks, as you've spent more and more time in Boston, Kellan and I have spent more and more time here. Sanding and painting and nailing and— well, you name it, we've done it. The house is nearly finished, and Kellan and I have talked it over. We think— no, we know for sure that June 19th is still the perfect day to begin the rest of our lives together. So, will you still be my wife, Susan? Will you spend the rest of your life with me? I know that the cabin isn't suited for a family of three, but we have this place now. The old Jacobson place, as your dad calls it. I think it'll do just fine."

Susan felt the tears roll down her cheeks as the reality of it all hit her. She threw her arms around him as she whispered, "You did this all for me?"

"Of course. You're everything to me. You're my entire world, Susan!" He breathed, then twirled her round and round in circles as her heart pumped and the joyous tears continued. She hadn't envisioned this, not in a million

A Vineyard Wedding

years. But Scott Frampton had always had a way of surprising her.

He led her through the house after that. Susan was mesmerized as she watched him position a key directly in the front door and actually open it, proof that it was theirs, that it may always be theirs.

Of course, the place hadn't yet been furnished, and there were still a number of design decisions to be made. Susan laughed and said, "You knew better than to make those without me, didn't you?" Scott affirmed that he did.

"It's not like me and Kel could ever pick out the perfect paint color for the bathroom, you know?" he said.

"Oh, I have a hunch. I saw Kellan pair orange with blue the other day," Susan said. "Besides, I'll need Lola and Christine's eye on everything. Oh, and Amanda will beg for wallpaper. She's such a stickler for that. She'll need her own room. And— oh, I'm getting ahead of myself."

"No, no. I want you to get ahead of yourself," Scott said. "I want this place to make you dream up all the different realities we'll have together here. We're still young, babe— only mid-forties. We still have forty years together to drive one another crazy."

Susan burst into laughter. She then traced a path through the foyer, past the newly-positioned cabinets in the kitchen, and out toward the porch, with its gorgeous view of the Vineyard Sound. If she peered through the trees off to the left just so, she could make out the outline of the Sheridan house.

It was beyond her wildest dreams to be so close to the ones she loved. Already, she could envision Baby Max— not such a baby any longer, barreling through the trees and hollering her name. What would Baby Max call her, anyway? Aunt Susie? Grandma Susie? They would cross that bridge when they came to it. And besides, labels weren't so important in the Sheridan family. There was so much love to go around.

Out on the porch, the waves rushed soundly across the white sands and basked against the edges of the white birch trees. Susan dropped her head against Scott's chest to listen to his beating heart. He reached into his backpack to draw out a bottle of red and two glasses.

"I want to toast to our future. Here at our new house."

But as he poured their glasses, Susan knew to do one thing before anything else.

She texted all of them: Amanda, Audrey, Christine, and Lola.

> SUSAN: The wedding is on. June 19th. Squash any and all rumors that it isn't moving forward, and get ready for the biggest party of your life. I'm marrying the love of my life! And best of all, we're moving into the Jacobson house next door!

By the time the text messages buzzed back through in response, Susan's lips were sealed over Scott's, and her mind was empty of any other thoughts. It was crazy how times could change and how they stayed the same. It was a remarkable thing.

Chapter Twenty

Susan, Amanda, and Marcie Shean sat together in one of the side offices outside of the courtroom. It was approximately twenty-five minutes prior to the start time of the next round of witness testimony. Susan had just finished explaining what had occurred on Martha's Vineyard with someone named "Marvin Stokes," a name that didn't ring any bells for Marcie Shean at all. In fact, Marcie seemed increasingly despondent. Susan sat across from her at the overly large table. Somehow, the girl seemed to have lost years from her face; she seemed more like seventeen, perhaps sixteen, on the verge of choosing her university and major of choice.

"I'm sorry. I don't know him. And I didn't really ever know any of those guys," Marcie whispered in that mouse-like voice of hers. "Freddy tried to keep everything separate from me. We had a bit of the money for a while, but yeah, Jimmy said that he definitely started using. I hated to sleep separately from him. I guess you could say we were co-dependent or something. I read a book about that once. We were textbook like that.

"But he never wanted the guys to come to the house. And I always worked while he did whatever he did to make enough money to use. Gosh, it sounds so crazy now, doesn't it? I just hate that it all came to this." Marcie's hands shook as she extended them over the table.

"The cops interviewed this Marvin guy and tracked down a few more witnesses for us," Susan explained. "I don't think we'll have time to see them today. The trial could extend a bit longer than expected. I hope you're up to that?"

"Whatever we need," Marcie replied, although her voice suggested that she was on the verge of some kind of mental break.

Amanda stood to go grab everyone cups of coffee. Her heels clacked off into the distance as she left Susan and Marcie alone. Marcie's eyes scanned the paintings that hung on the wall in the large room. Sometimes, Susan hated how intimidating courthouses seemed. It was all this pomp and circumstance for nothing.

"I can't believe he went all the way to the Vineyard to find you," Marcie said suddenly. "How awful it must have been."

Susan nodded. "Stuff like this happened before when I used to work with my ex-husband, but we had a good system in place. A system of protection that I thought the Vineyard would also provide, out there on that rock in the middle of the ocean. I was wrong to assume that, though, and have definitely learned my lesson."

"But you shouldn't take cases like mine anymore," Marcie said. "You have so much to live for— a beautiful family. Everyone on the island knows about the Sheridans and what kind of people you are. There was no reason you should have helped me. But I think my dad knew you would. He sensed that you'd know you were our last hope."

A lump formed in Susan's throat. She reached across the table and cupped the girl's hand tenderly. Pain beamed off of her, torment of the worst kind. This girl, this poor girl, had discovered her dead boyfriend on the floor of the apartment they had shared. Susan had never gone through anything worse. Assuredly, the girl would have nightmares surrounding that very moment for the rest of her days. It was like a poison that could never be released.

There was a loud rap at the door. Susan glanced at the clock, which told her they still had seventeen minutes till the start of the session. She released the girl's hand and stepped toward the door. When she opened it, she found herself face-to-face with the bailiff.

"The judge would like to speak with you in his chambers," he told her.

Susan left Marcie with two of the guards. She traced a path back toward the chambers, where she found the prosecution's lawyer, Paul, waiting. He looked irritated, and he wasn't sure where to put his hands. When Susan greeted him, he didn't say anything in return.

Once in the chambers, the judge folded his hands over the desk and looked at them with eyes that clearly indicated he was irritated.

"I've just gotten word from the police station. One of the men connected to Marvin Stokes just confessed to the murder of Freddy Peterson."

Susan gasped, then turned her eyes toward Paul, who furrowed his brow and said, "Are you sure about this?"

"Quite sure," the judge affirmed. "We will make a formal announcement once the session begins. At that time, I will allow for Marcie Shean's immediate release. She will be free to go."

Susan felt as though she had slept-walked out into the hallway. Once there, she peered up at Paul, who looked strangely flabbergasted.

"This is such amazing news! Freddy's parents will finally know what really happened," Susan said.

Paul scoffed. "Sure. Now they know he was a drug-addled lunatic involved with all the wrong people."

"Isn't the truth better than sending an innocent girl to prison?" Susan asked, her voice laced with snark.

"It is. Congratulations, Miss Sheridan. All the best to you and your client," Paul returned as he walked out toward the courtroom in defeat.

Minutes later, Amanda found Susan and Marcie out on the wooden bench. Susan hadn't yet found the words to explain the news to Marcie. Her heart hummed with fear and excitement. Amanda pressed a cup of coffee into her hand and said, "Sorry. The line was so long." Susan hardly heard her.

The judge entered. He blasted his gavel against the top of the large desk and announced, "Today in the proceedings of the State Versus Marcie Shean, I find the defendant not guilty. The trial is dismissed."

A gasp erupted across the room. Marcie's eyes bugged from her skull. She gripped Susan's hand there on the bench, and Susan could feel how quick her pulse was. It raced like a rabbit's.

"What did you do?" Marcie demanded then.

Susan shook her head. "There was a confession."

Marcie's eyes filled with tears. "They got the guy. They got the guy who did it."

"It seems like it."

A Vineyard Wedding

Tears rolled down Marcie's cheeks. One of the guards came and removed her handcuffs. She shook her wrists around and eased one hand over her opposite wrist to soothe the skin. After a pause, she turned around to look her father in the eye. It was difficult to decipher what the two of them thought there at that moment. Her father nodded firmly and then gestured toward the back exit. It was time to return home.

Susan walked with Marcie toward the entrance. Everywhere they looked, cameras flashed toward them. Microphones were shoved toward their mouths as journalists hollered, "MARCIE! Now that you're deemed not guilty, do you have something to say to the entire city of Boston, a city that was entirely sure of your guilt until now?"

"Marcie! What would you say to Freddy right now if you could?"

"Marcie!"

"Marcie, wait!"

Susan wrapped an arm around her client and hustled her out toward the sidewalk, where she hurriedly hailed a cab. Together, Amanda, Marcie, and Susan pressed themselves into the back seat. Marcie's father had been caught by a journalist, who peppered him with questions on the sidewalk. Marcie furrowed her brow.

"He's my ride."

"We can take you back to the island. If you like," Susan said.

Marcie nodded. "Just text him if you can. Tell him I'm okay. And I'll see him at home."

* * *

Within the hour, Susan watched as Marcie draped her head against the car seat headrest there in the passenger seat of her vehicle. She had soft rock purring on the radio, and already, Audrey was fast asleep in the backseat. It was as though all the trauma of the previous weeks had built up around them and reminded them of their own exhaustion.

Still, as they drove toward the Vineyard, Susan hummed with questions. The girl had the rest of her life stretched out before her. What on earth did that feel like?

"Marcie. Can I ask you something?"

Marcie turned her eyes the slightest bit toward Susan, proof that she listened in.

"What does it feel like? Now that it's over?"

Marcie chewed on her bottom lip before answering. "I don't know. It's difficult to describe. I was pretty set on spending my life in prison, to be honest. I had a strategy in my head about how I would live out each decade. And now, it's like, I've been given this new gift of what feels like eternal life. I don't want to mess it up, you know? And that's even more pressure."

Susan chuckled. "That's a funny problem to have, isn't it?"

Marcie nodded. After a long pause, she turned her eyes to watch the road as it rushed past. "When I first met Freddy, we talked non-stop about how we wanted to discover the world together. We would make out in the walk-in fridge at the restaurant and talk about our daydreams. He said he would show me the world. I don't know why I believed him because, hell, he'd never seen the world himself. But all I had known was Martha's Vineyard. I was swept up in the idea of it all. But before I knew it, we were arguing, and there wasn't any money, and we were screaming at each other and— well. But I still loved him, you know. I never stopped loving him, even when I would tell him I wanted to leave him. He always begged me to stay. Gosh, I wish I had left. I would never have gotten involved in all of this. But I don't know where I would have gone."

Susan adjusted her hands low on the steering wheel at five and seven. If Amanda had woken, she would have given her mother a hard time about this. She always did.

"Do you think you'll stay on the island now that it's over?"

Marcie shook her head quickly. "I want to go where nobody has ever heard my name. Maybe a different country. Somewhere in South America. Maybe I can learn how to dance the tango. Or paint really well. Or ride a horse."

Susan's heart swelled at all these beautiful images. She could just make it out— Marcie, wearing a vibrant smile, maybe even introducing herself with a new name, with a fresh accent. Maybe she would learn to speak Spanish or Portuguese. Maybe it would be enough just to be alone somewhere new, a place where she could stew over her thoughts and process them. A place where she could mourn the death of Freddy Peterson, a man she'd loved, and a man she now probably regretted she'd loved so much.

"You're going to get through this, Marcie," Susan told her softly. "You're a writer on the first page of the draft called 'the rest of your life.' It's up to you to write the first sentence."

"That's beautiful," Marcie replied. "And I think I've had enough bad luck for now. Maybe I'll find some good luck over the next horizon. Who knows?"

"Who knows," Susan echoed.

"Ah, but you know, the first thing I want to do is this."

"What's that?" Susan asked.

Marcie drew herself up from the headrest and exhaled slowly. "I want to swim in the Nantucket Sound. I want to feel the ocean up to my neck and then dunk myself under. I want to hear only the sound of my heartbeat as I swim through the ocean waves. As an island girl, that was the only thing I knew for years and years."

Susan blinked back tears. When she'd been a wife and a mother in Newark, she had always had similar dreams about the ocean. It was true what they said that wherever you went, you carried Martha's Vineyard with you. It was a part of you.

"I hope you'll look me up when you visit your brother and father," Susan said. "I want to hear about every adventure and every wild romance."

Marcie gave her a sheepish smile. "Okay. I'll see you, but I can't say it'll be soon."

Chapter Twenty-One

Susan stopped the engine outside of the Sheridan house. She looked at the house with suspicion. After all, news of the end of the trial had certainly reached the airwaves, and it wasn't like the Sheridans to let any such major event pass by without some sort of celebration. Still, Susan prayed they would back off, at least for a few days. It had all been overwhelming, an emotional rollercoaster. Her head still spun, and her stomach ached with nausea. This was what it meant to be "back in the world of criminal law." She remembered it well, now.

Amanda was wordless as they entered the cozy house. She had slept nearly all the way back from Boston, and her motions seemed slow and sluggish. She snapped on the light in the mudroom as she removed her kitten heels and flashed her hair around her back.

Susan stepped through the hallway. When she reached the little breakfast nook, her heart surged at the sight of a beautifully decorated cake, one straight from the artistic eye of one Christine Sheridan. It was dotted with raspberries and flecks of white chocolate, and she'd written, in perfect icing-cursive, the word: CONGRATULATIONS. Susan splayed a hand across her chest as emotions overwhelmed her.

And when she turned to face the living room, one by one, Christine, Lola, Audrey, Baby Max, Wes, Scott, and even Kellan appeared. They'd hidden behind the couch and the chairs. They didn't spout any kind of "SURPRISE"; they didn't scream. They just rushed toward her and Amanda and covered them with hugs and congratulations.

"You did so well. What a remarkable thing!" Grandpa Wes beamed.

"It wasn't all us," Susan said. "The actual murderer eventually confessed. He—"

"Come on," Christine said with a cheeky grin. "We know all the effort you put in. You basically smoked out the villain in the story. The police had no idea what they were doing until you started sniffing around."

Amanda nudged Susan playfully. "It's true. Mom is basically a lawyer-turned-spy."

Scott hustled up and placed a kiss on her lips, then wrapped his firm arms around her. Everything within her wanted to yank him upstairs, if only so she could huddle against him and allow him to hold her and finally fall into the mindlessness of sleep.

But cake would do, at least for a while.

They sat in the last of the evening sunlight near the water, each with a plate of cake. Out in the distance, sailboats chased one another like wild cats while their sails caught the frenetic energy of the last light. Susan sat between Scott's legs and leaned against his chest, listening to the familiar sound of her family's conversation.

"Boston is up in arms, you know," Lola said. "They just can't believe that girl is innocent. They had it so sure in their heads that she was the killer."

"People love a good story like that," Christine agreed. "Difficult to show people the truth."

"What will Marcie do now?" Grandpa Wes asked.

"She says she has about a million plans, but all of them still seem fictional to her," Susan said.

"If I was her, I would just run all over the world. Freedom must feel so delicious right now," Christine said.

"She won't waste that feeling. I know that for sure," Susan said.

Very soon, the conversation leaned toward other topics. Susan nibbled at the last crumbs of her cake as Christine brought up the fact that it was already June 3rd, which meant that the island's favorite couple would soon marry. Susan's heart leaped into her throat. There was still so much to be done.

Lola laughed. "If we had left everything up to you, that wedding would have never happened."

Susan, who was a well-known control freak, arched an eyebrow. "What do you mean?"

"Well, we had a chat with Charlotte about all of this a few weeks ago, and she sprung into action," Christine said. "You remember how quickly she works. That Ursula wedding at Thanksgiving came together like a frantic whirlwind. Because the island knows and cares about you already, it was no trouble at all."

"And Claire is going all out with the flowers. Jeez. She's arranged so many potential bouquets, it's ridiculous," Lola affirmed.

Susan wasn't sure quite what to say. She turned her head slightly to catch Scott's eye. "I can't believe it. I get to marry the love of my life, and I hardly had to lift a finger thanks to my amazing family."

"We knew it was stressing you out," Lola told her.

"The only thing you need to do, I guess, is go back and get that dress!" Christine cried. "I already called her, and she said it's still there, waiting for you. All that history, waiting to add to your story."

* * *

Back up on the porch, Christine disappeared and reappeared a few minutes later, armed with one of the old, slightly-stained books from Anna's chest of treasures. She lifted the book as the conversation with the others died around her.

"I found this passage in Mom's diary the other day. I couldn't believe it. I feel like it's the perfect time to read it if you'll let me."

Susan nodded as her throat tightened. "Please."

"Here I am, a young girl on the brink of becoming a woman," Christine read. "For tomorrow, I will walk down the aisle to meet the love of my life— Wesley Sheridan, and become one of the Sheridan clan. The entire concept is beyond my wildest dreams. And isn't it funny? All those years, you dream and ache to become a wife, to belong to someone, as a girl. When it finally lands in your lap, it seems to be one of the most terrifying events of your life. You don't realize the finality of it all when you're eight or nine, donning whatever lace blanket is around and walking slowly through your parents' living room. You don't realize the severity of 'till death do us part.'

"But when I look into Wesley Sheridan's eyes, I feel that I know something. I know something about our future. I can practically feel our babies kicking around in my belly. I imagine he'll care for me when I'm sick; that we'll fight over money troubles and then find a way through; that we'll ache with sadness and longing as we grow older and develop wrinkles and find new and interesting ways to love one another.

"For this is what I believe a marriage truly is: I believe it means opening your eyes every day to a person who is also in the midst of ever-constant change. And it means loving the bits that are still there, along with the bits that they've left behind, along with the bits that they're headed towards. Time isn't linear; love is complex. And I am so open to the concept of loving Wesley Sheridan completely, for all the days of my life."

Susan's eyes snapped closed as emotion swept over her like a forceful wave. Scott squeezed her hand hard. Always, Susan had known her mother to be a poetic genius, a woman of tremendous thought and feeling. Hearing these words was incredible; it also made her heart quake with sadness. What sorts of things might she had said, now, had she been allowed to live past the age of thirty-eight? Would she have taken any of that back? Would she have laughed at her youthfulness?

"She really did, though," Wes breathed then.

Susan blinked up to find her father in the midst of his own tears of longing.

"She loved me all the days of her life. We all know that love is complicated, but I felt her love for me and, indeed, her love for the three of you girls in everything else she did. She was a powerful woman who made me proud to call her my wife. She wanted to know and feel and do everything."

"I can feel it in her words," Lola whispered. "I only wish she could be here with us."

Susan reached across the table to grip Lola's hand. Christine's hand joined theirs.

"She is here with us," Wes said finally. "I see her in everything you girls are. I see her in Audrey's laughter. I see her in Susan's quick wit and perseverance. I see her in Lola's creativity and great style, and I see her in Christine's glorious smile and ability to change and grow. And Amanda, I see her in your cooking. Some of the new experiments you craft in that kitchen remind me of when Anna would say, 'Dang it, Wes, I can't eat the same stuff every day. My palate gets so bored.'" Wes chuckled inwardly.

Kellan lifted his glass of lemonade. "She sounds like a really remarkable woman. I wish I could have met her."

"She was," Scott said. "I'm so glad I knew her when I did."

Susan's heart swelled again. Wasn't it remarkable that the man she would soon marry had witnessed that part of her life, that wonderful and innocent time when her mother had lived on at that house and worked at the Sunrise Cove? He'd known her then, and he knew her now. It was such a gift that people could see you through so many different eras of your life without judgment and with seemingly endless amounts of love.

Chapter Twenty-Two

Susan draped a pearl necklace around her neck and clasped it just at the nape. Each individual pearl caught the light from the lamp and beamed it back into the antique mirror before her. As she took in the sight, she very nearly tricked her mind into seeing herself as Anna Sheridan— the previous owner of this piece of jewelry— especially as she'd witnessed Anna putting the pearls around her slender neck countless times.

This time, Susan had wanted to bring a piece of her mother along with her for the rehearsal dinner. Somehow, it was already June 18th and in only twenty-four hours, she would marry the love of her life.

Downstairs, Amanda hollered that it was nearly time to go. Susan stepped up to get a better full-body view of her entire ensemble. She had gone with a cream-colored dress for the rehearsal, semi-low cut, with a beautiful view of her feminine shoulders. She and Amanda had picked it out on a recent trip to New York, which they'd called her "bachelorette" weekend. Mostly, they'd just shopped and chatted about the legal system. They had both agreed that nearly anyone else in the history of the world would have thought the time being spent was boring, but it was perfect for them. "Like mother, like daughter."

On the trip to New York, Susan had asked Amanda again about her failed marriage to Chris. "Does it still bother you? That he left?"

Amanda's answer had surprised Susan.

"To be honest, Mom, not at all. I feel like it should bother me more, but sometimes I have to force myself to remember that it could have been a lot worse if we had actually gone through with everything. I can't even imagine if we did, where we would be in five years— probably at city hall getting a divorce. I'm just glad I dodged that bullet."

Susan smiled at her daughter. She knew Amanda was right.

The rehearsal was held at the event space itself— the Harbor View Hotel in Edgartown, a historic, landmark hotel built in 1891, with a beautiful view of the lighthouse, a charming gazebo, and sweeping lawns with every assortment of flowers. Scott and Kellan arrived just in the nick of time— both gasping for breath as they buttoned their suit jackets.

"Sorry. We've been working on the house all day," Scott said. "Kellan pointed out the time, so we rushed around, getting ready."

"We both took two-minute showers," Kellan announced proudly.

Susan laughed. "I can't wait to see everything you've done!"

In the wake of Scott's showing her the house, she and her sisters had selected a number of paint colors and wall-

A Vineyard Wedding

paper samplings. This would all come after she, Scott, and Kellan moved into the property itself, probably the following week. Scott finalized the last of it and had even begun to move in bits and pieces of furniture to ensure that they were comfortable as they got the rest of their lives together. "There's no rush," Susan had told him several times. "We'll just piece it together as we go."

The rehearsal went off without a hitch, and then the bridal party returned to the Sunrise Cove Bistro for the rehearsal dinner. Zach Walters had arranged for a usual Zach Walters menu, although even from outside the bistro, Susan sensed that he'd given it one hundred and ten percent. He had even placed a large placard outside, which listed the menu for the evening. It listed lobster tails with chive butter, brie with crab and macaroni, seared scallops and spiced pomegranate glaze, hazelnut glazed cauliflower, which he'd called "steak for vegetarians," and beef Steak Wellington for everyone else. Zach hadn't allowed Susan to know a single element about the evening's dinner menu, and Susan was glad she'd allowed him to surprise her. She whistled as Amanda performed a slow clap.

"Zach is simply the best at what he does," Amanda praised. "But how much do you want to bet he's back there having a hissy fit about one problem or another?"

"You know it's true," Susan said with a laugh. "All chefs have tempers. Glad I don't work with them."

The bistro itself had been set up with several long tables; white table clothes caught the glow of flickering candles, and lilies adorned the spaces between the ornate plates. Already, many members of the Sheridan and Montgomery families had arrived, along with Lily and Sarah and their families and a few members of Scott's party. Scott didn't have much family any longer, but he had been an islander his entire life and thusly, his collection of friends was enough and filled with love.

Uncle Trevor waved a sturdy hand as Susan entered. "There's our beautiful bride!" He stepped over and placed a kiss on her cheek. Susan remembered over a year ago when she had come to the island for the first time after so long. That fateful day, Uncle Trevor had been the one to pick her up from the ferry. He had been the first set of eyes she'd seen from her past. She would never forget the intensity of that moment. How finally, she realized she was home.

Zach appeared at the door between the kitchen and the bistro. Christine was behind him, red-faced but smiling. She whipped around him as he cried, "Christine! I still need your help!" But she hurried toward Susan and hugged her tight.

"I told Zach over and over again that I would hire someone else for this event," Susan said with a funny smile.

"You know how he is. He lives for this," Christine said. "But everything is nearly done, so he should be able to eat with us while the rest of the staff takes over for the rest of the courses. It was just a lot of prep work. I can't stress that enough. We've been awake for a long time."

"How are you feeling?" Susan asked.

"Oh, you know. Pregnant, I guess." Christine laughed as she rolled a hand over her still flat stomach. "But the morning sickness seems to be clearing up. I shouldn't say that, though. Every time I say that, it comes back with a vengeance."

"Oh yeah. It can definitely hear you." This was Audrey, who seemed to appear from nowhere. She held

Baby Max in her left arm, and he sucked frantically on a pacifier as his large blue eyes caught the candlelight. She was dressed beautifully, in a black dress that revealed what was probably too much leg for a family occasion (although who was Susan to say?).

"You look hot," Audrey said to both Amanda and Susan, who laughed in return.

"Thanks. Glad to know I can still look hot at forty-five," Susan said.

Charlotte hustled up to announce that all spaces were accounted for. She was totally in her element, clutching a clipboard, her eyes alight.

"Charlotte. You promise me you'll sit with all of us? Enjoy yourself?" Susan asked. "You've done such a marvelous job at arranging everything, but this is just the rehearsal. We sit. We eat. Maybe someone will make a speech. Not a whole lot more to do."

Charlotte heaved a sigh. "I know. And to be honest with you, I hired an assistant to take over a lot of the responsibilities tomorrow. I just couldn't bear the thought of watching all of you have fun together while I had to work."

"Thank goodness," Susan said. "I want you there on the dance floor with me until our knees give out, which might be nine-thirty. We are in our forties now."

Charlotte howled with laughter as Susan and Scott weaved their way toward the head of one of the long tables. Amanda was positioned to the left of Susan, while Jake and Kristen sat near Kellan. Apparently, they'd decided to leave the twins with a babysitter that night, there at the Sunrise Cove. The twins would be at the ceremony the following day, but then, the same babysitter would take over so that Jake and Kristen could enjoy the festivities. It would be one of their final trips together as a family of only four. Soon, even more madness would begin.

The meal was absolutely extraordinary. Throughout, Zach beamed and whispered to Christine, speaking just loud enough for Susan to hear a few chairs down. "I think the chives really come through on the butter," for example, or, "Wow, the scallops really turned out this time. Better than that event last week. Remember, didn't I say, Christine, that that was the warm-up event for tonight?"

Grandpa Wes sat on the other side of Kellan, next to his sister Kerry, and across from Uncle Trevor. As they finished their third course, one of the hired wait staff approached to pour another bit of wine into Wes's glass. As the waiter stepped away, Wes clinked his glass with the side of his fork. Conversation dimmed around him as he stood. He lifted his glass toward Susan as his eyes glowed with love and gratitude.

"I just want to say a few words before we proceed with this absolutely incredible meal," Wes said. "Susan? You were my first child—my baby girl. When you were born, I had the funniest feeling that I would have done anything for you. I would have moved mountains for you. I still would, you know, although the old back strength isn't what it used to be.

"But still. I want to say some words. Here and now. I know I'm an older man, and I know I've missed so much of your life. But I don't think I can possibly say just how grateful I am to be here to watch you marry the love of your life. Even though we fell apart for many years, you've always been the sparkle in my eye, my beautiful daughter. You've made me prouder than words. I only wish your mother was here to watch you walk down that aisle tomorrow. I wish you and Scott the most beautiful life together. After all, you are Susan Sheridan. And anyone who is anyone on the island of Martha's Vineyard knows that Susan Sheridan gets what she wants— every single time. Welcome to the family, Scott. I'm so happy to be able to officially call you my son-in-law."

Wes lifted his glass higher as all members of the rehearsal dinner followed suit.

"We love you, Scott and Susan. Here's to the rest of your life," he said.

Chapter Twenty-Three

When Susan awoke on the morning of her wedding, only the softest of light smeared itself across the Vineyard Sound horizon line, and most of the island remained lost in sleep. She padded downstairs toward the kitchen to discover it empty. She looked out the window to the rolling hills and water below and could feel the corners of her mouth turn upward as she thought, *today is the big day*. She would marry the man she'd always loved and take on his name, the Frampton name, for good.

But she wasn't surprised to know that she wasn't the only one awake at the Sheridan house. After all, it was the central heartbeat of so much family. There, on the counter, sat a full pot of piping hot coffee. And through the window that opened out onto the porch, she spotted the gray outline of one Wes Sheridan, who assuredly stood to watch the first of the morning waves roll in from the Sound. Susan exhaled somberly. It was somehow strange to feel this way at forty-five. She felt as though she had to say goodbye to her childhood home all over again, although she would really only be next door.

The screen door screeched as she entered the porch with her own mug of coffee. When Wes shifted his weight toward her, she spotted a funny sight in his arms. He was cradling a sleeping Max, who wore a light blue sleep jumpsuit. His eyelashes were so long and delicate, splayed across his cheeks, and his lips looked on the verge of dropping his pacifier.

"He was crying upstairs, so I managed to get to him just as Audrey got up," Wes explained. "I told her to go back to sleep. She needs it, I think. As much as she pretends she's all right, she's still just as exhausted as any new mom."

Susan placed a hand on her father's shoulder. "I know you mean the world to Audrey. And this little guy already loves you so much. Look at how peaceful he is."

Wes beamed, even as his eyes grew shadowed. The silence enveloped them for a moment until Wes cleared his throat and murmured, "I didn't want to say this as much last night, but I have an addendum to my speech."

Susan's throat constricted as his eyes connected with hers. She didn't dare speak.

"I don't know how much longer I'll be around," Wes said finally.

Susan furrowed her brow. This wasn't the kind of conversation she wanted to have. Not now. Not ever.

But still— she wanted to be the type of daughter to allow Wes to say such things if he needed to. She couldn't refute that. She had felt the potential pain of dying only last year, as cancer had attempted to swallow her whole. She had wanted to say such things to Amanda, but she'd held back as she'd fought harder. Dementia wasn't really something you could fight; it came after you little by little. It was like the story of the tortoise and the hare. The tortoise always won in the end— as did time.

"I know that's difficult for you to hear. But it's not as difficult for me to say it," Wes said. "I feel that God gave me a tremendous gift in bringing you girls back home to me. I have to come to terms with the fact that the Sheridan line will continue to grow and change and mold. It will grow stronger, even in my absence. I just want to soak in the last of it all that I can. And dammit, I can't believe I can finally walk one of my girls down the aisle."

Susan's eyes welled with tears. She dropped her head upon her father's chest, to the right of Baby Max. His firm arm wrapped around her shoulder as the first of what would probably be many sobs over the course of the day escaped her. There was no escaping this inevitability. They could only live in their gratefulness.

Charlotte had set aside one of the more beautiful rooms of the Harbor View Hotel for the girls' pre-wedding preparation. The wedding was set to begin at four-thirty, with cocktails immediately after, before another incredible meal and hours and hours of dancing. They had selected a number of Vineyard-based bands to perform before a local DJ planned to take over around ten-thirty. Already, the space outside was decorated immaculately with nearly three hundred chairs lining the aisle, glorious white lilies opening their wide arms toward the sky, and a beautiful, wooden-carved arc, beneath which Scott and Susan would say their vows. Charlotte had really outdone herself.

"But she always outdoes herself," Lola said then as she leaned toward the mirror and smeared a bit of eyeliner over the top of her right eyelid. "If you told her to chill out once, she would probably lose her mind."

"That's the same with all of us, isn't it?" Christine said as she stepped into her lavender dress. There, with her stomach exposed, you could make out the slightest of baby bumps. When she buttoned the delicate pearl buttons on the back of the dress, however, the baby bump disappeared without a trace beneath the flowing satin.

Audrey appeared in the room after that. She'd already donned her own lavender dress; her hair flowed beautifully, but her lips were coated with what looked to be donut icing.

"Where have you been, Missy?" Lola asked as she reached for a wet wipe— an essential tool at any wedding.

Audrey shrugged. "Jennifer Conrad from the Frosted Delights just arrived with a ton of donuts for the bridal party."

"What!" Amanda jumped up from the corner, then placed her hand over her stomach. "On second thought, I don't want to be bloated for the pictures."

"Oh, come on. You can have a donut. It's a celebration," Christine said as she hustled toward the door. "I'll grab enough for all of us."

Susan remained seated. She'd only just slipped on the antique wedding dress, the same one worn by a film star of the forties, and she feasted on her reflection, knowing that all too soon, this moment would slip away. It was a funny thing about getting older; looks mattered less and less, it was true— but you were also more aware of what you needed to appreciate. If only she could go back in time and tell her teenage self not to worry so much about having "washboard abs," which she'd tried for, tearing through the pages of *Seventeen* magazine for "top tips." What a waste it had all been. She was already beautiful.

Amanda appeared behind her. She touched some of the delicate curls along her mother's shoulder and said, "You look really beautiful, you know." The words were so tender that they nearly broke Susan's heart.

"It's strange. I don't remember feeling like this when I married your father," Susan said. "I suppose I was just worried about you and Jake at the time. You were both so young and wild. I wanted everything in your lives to be perfect, but now, you and Jake are grown. Jake has a whole family of his own. So now, this decision is all about me, my life, and my own happiness."

Amanda nodded. "And you think you're making the right choice?"

"Absolutely. It is both imperfect and perfect at the same time. As all wonderful things are," Susan said.

Just before four-thirty, Susan, Amanda, Audrey, Lola, and Christine gathered near the side entrance of the hotel, where double-wide doors would lead them out toward the massive Vineyard crowd, which had gathered for the wedding of the Vineyard-famous Susan Sheridan. Throughout the previous year, everyone had pulled for them in all things as they had watched as Susan had powered through cancer, as Scott had fixed up the Inn, and as their love had grown into something so strong that it even shocked them.

It had been rather difficult to decide who to invite. Thusly, they'd gone with almost everyone. And nearly everyone had RSVPed "yes."

Wes appeared in the hallway wearing a beautiful tux, and his hair had been styled wonderfully, with a part off to the side. It was remarkable how little hair he'd lost over the years; it was remarkable that his smile seemed just as youthful as ever before. As he took in the view of Susan in her wedding gown, his eyes filled with tears.

"It's better than I ever imagined," he said. "You look so much like your mother right now. It's uncanny. But you also look like yourself, my unique and beautiful Susan Sheridan." He knelt and gave her a delicate kiss on the cheek just as the string quintet outside started. It was time for the girls to begin their steady walk down the aisle. It was time for Susan to finally become a Frampton, after so many years of wishing.

Audrey led the charge, a traditional Aries girl. She soaked up the first of the attention and led Lola, then Christine, then Amanda, who was, naturally, Susan's maid of honor. As Susan walked down the aisle, she made eye contact with several islanders she adored— her cousin, Claire, and her husband Russell; Claire's twins, Abby and Gail; Camilla Jenkins, who worked at the hospital; Chelsea, Olivia Hesson's daughter, who worked at the diner; Nancy Remington, Neal Remington's widow, whom Susan had gotten to know over the previous year. Her heart surged with love for all of them.

But soon, her eyes had room only for Scott.

Scott and Kellan had opted for near-matching tuxedos. Kellan stood alongside his father proudly, with his chest puffed out. Scott shifted his weight, proof of his nervousness, but maintained heavy eye contact with Susan. With every step she took, her mind purred with ideas of her luck. He was the most handsome, kindest man she'd ever known, and he would be with her forever. Why did she deserve this? She supposed she would never truly know.

Scott extended his hands to allow Susan to drop hers over them. There seemed to be lightning between their skin. The pastor they'd hired to perform the ceremony, a man called Randall, stepped closer to them as the string quintet died down off to the side.

"Good afternoon, everyone, and welcome to a most auspicious occasion. We here on the island of Martha's Vineyard know and love Susan Sheridan and Scott Frampton. We know them to be honorable, hard-working, kind, considerate, and prosperous people, and today, we have been given the privilege to watch them marry. Lucky us."

The crowd chuckled. Scott's eyes filled with tears. Susan told herself to hold off on hers— to stay in the moment as long as she could.

But the moment Scott began his vows, which he had written himself, she knew she was a goner.

"Susan. From the moment I laid eyes on you thirty years ago, I knew my life wouldn't be the same. We were just teenagers, but you already taught me new ways to think to feel, and I had this sense that I needed to always be better and work harder, if only to be good enough for you.

"Our paths to here were long, winding roads that finally connected once again. I know that the woman I see before me today has mountains of history; I have my own history, too. But that history has made us who we are today— two people with even more love than we had beforehand, who've overcome countless obstacles to unite once more. Susan Sheridan, I love you more than I can possibly describe. And I thank my lucky stars every day that you want to be my wife and join me and Kellan on our life journeys."

Susan felt the waterworks. She brushed away a tear before it threatened to roll all the way down her cheek and muss her makeup. When she spoke, her voice wavered; she wasn't sure she could trust herself to get to the end.

"Scott. One afternoon, when I was sixteen years old, you appeared at the dock beneath my house in a boat and said, 'Come with me.' You refused to tell me where we were going. I was hesitant, of course, but so glad that I took that chance and went along with you. That day allowed me to learn that you were the type of boy that I wanted to fall in love with, the type of man I wanted to spend the rest of my life with. And my sisters reminded me of that every single day for a very long time."

The crowd chuckled. It seemed clear that not a single member of the audience hadn't given over to tears yet.

"You took me beneath the cliffs, and you held my hands in yours and you said, 'Susan, I'm going to marry you one day.' And I remember what I said. I said— only if you have a five-year plan."

Scott laughed outright as everyone else joined in.

"You were totally shocked. You'd wanted it to be this romantic afternoon, but I had given you a dose of reality. At least, I had thought I'd given you that. For, what I know now is this. You can make up as many five-year plans as you want, but you never really know what will happen next. You have to take each day as it is. And you have to love as hard as you can along the way. Right now, I'm a cancer survivor. I'm a divorcée. I'm a mother and a lawyer. I'm a sister, a daughter, and a friend. And I can't wait to be your wife as we wade through the rest of our life together. I love you, Scott Frampton."

Moments later, the pastor pronounced them man and

wife, and they kissed with the zealous energy of their teenage selves, despite living out their lives in their forties. The quintet began to play again as they rushed back down the aisle. Both were out of breath, gasping, as they finished up near the drink area and grabbed two glasses of champagne. They clinked their glasses together as they made heavy eye contact.

"Here's to the rest of our lives," Susan said.

"And to one of the greatest parties this island will ever see," Scott said mischievously.

Chapter Twenty-Four

And it was— one of the greatest parties, that is. The island of Martha's Vineyard spun with light and love as anyone who was anyone rushed to the drink table, shimmied across the dance floor, gossiped and laughed and took chances and risks that would be often talked about for the rest of the summer and into the fall. Susan tried her best to take it all in.

There, off to the right, Lola and Tommy danced with vibrant smiles as Tommy's broad hand stretched out on her lower back. Susan wondered if Tommy would ever take the plunge and actually ask beautiful Lola to marry him. Perhaps neither were really the type to settle down, no matter how much Susan wanted them to smack a label on it. Then, off to the left, Zach and Christine laughed and bantered together as Christine drank sparkling water with a slice of lemon. Throughout Christine's life on the Vineyard, Susan had watched as her drinking had lightened up— until now, of course, when she had to fully abstain from it. "I don't miss it at all," Christine had told Susan the previous week. "All my life, it seemed like alcohol would be a constant. Now, I look around, and I feel the immensity of all of your love. And I don't need it. It's a funny thing. But it makes me want to cry for previous versions of myself, who thought that alcohol was the only way to feel comfortable."

Amanda and Sam palled around together throughout the reception. Amanda was rosy-cheeked and lovely, and she looked far more energetic than her reserved, Type-A personality normally allowed. Sam was handsome and cracking jokes that made Amanda double over with laughter. When Susan passed by, she said, "Are you okay? You look like you're in pain." To this, Amanda replied, "I just can't stop laughing."

Audrey had passed Max off on a babysitter within the hotel, and now, she'd made up her mind to dance the night away with Noah. The pair was incredibly handsome together, bright lights of youthfulness. Once Noah lifted Audrey off the ground like some kind of *Dirty Dancing* trick, everyone oohed and ahhed as Audrey squealed with delight.

"They're trying to steal our show," Scott pointed out with a laugh.

"You want to try doing that with me?" Susan asked.

"If you want tonight to end at the hospital, we can give it a shot," Scott said, flashing her a playful grin.

Naturally, the food was spectacular. It had all been arranged by Zach, who'd ultimately recommended another high-caliber chef, who'd arrived from Boston early that morning to get started on everything. "He's the best of the best, besides me, of course," he'd said before adding, "I really would have done this wedding for you, Susan, but Christine says she doesn't want all the stress of, well, my stress."

Susan was mesmerized at Zach's ability to actually listen for a change. He and Christine had been through a great deal over the previous months. He'd left for a time after Baby Max's illness, as the entire situation had reminded him so much of his daughter's death. Therapy and time had helped. Love would be the answer, as it always had been before.

Around eleven, the crowd gathered at the edge of one of the docks nearest the hotels as Scott carried Susan over the top of his speedboat. He placed her delicately back to the ground and placed a kiss on her lips as the crowd roared. Lola and Christine had even decorated the back of the boat with a large banner that read: JUST MARRIED. Susan, who had drunk a few glasses of wine, grinned sheepishly at the massive crowd and waved like the excited bride she was.

"Thank you all!" she cried as Scott revved up the engine. "We love you so much!"

Scott sped them out beyond the lighthouse before motoring westward, back toward Oak Bluffs. Susan told him to go slowly, as she wanted to lean back and enjoy the amazing splay of stars above. They seemed so dense above them, so many that it was impossible to count. They twinkled down, lending their blessing.

It no longer scared Susan to be out on a boat at night. She'd once feared it after the death of her mother. But the death had been an accident, and she trusted Scott with her whole being. He would never do anything to put her in danger.

Scott pulled the boat up to the newly built dock beneath what had once been the Jacobson house. It was a funny thing to park here— just about a hundred feet from where the Sheridan dock rested. Susan told her heart,

"*This is your new home,*" as she watched Scott tie up the rope and lead her up onto the dock.

The Jacobson house was decorated with what seemed to be hundreds of glowing lights. The pathway up from the dock was lined with them, as was the porch that overlooked the water. The porch itself flickered with candlelight— proof that Scott had hired someone to come decorate the place and prepare it for their first night as husband and wife.

As they walked from the porch, a line of rose petals led them through the fully-renovated kitchen, past the newly constructed fireplace, and toward the staircase. With each step, Susan could feel the immensity of their future together. She could see them huddled by the fire in conversation. She could see them cooking together, dreaming together. She could see them in swimsuits, even as they aged, gardening around the sides of the house and making one another mojitos. She could feel it all.

And it hadn't even happened yet. She would be allowed the entire ride.

Upstairs, Scott had positioned a large bed at the center of the bedroom. There wasn't a single other piece of furniture, only this. And as she turned toward him to kiss him for the first time in their new house, he said, "Well, hello, Mrs. Frampton. I have been waiting for this moment for thirty years."

It was time for their lives to begin.

* * *

Susan and Scott walked hand-in-hand the following late morning as they weaved through the thick trees that lined the space between their home and the Sheridan house.

Susan felt light as a feather; she hadn't had even a moment's headache in the morning, and she'd brewed a pot of coffee and eaten a baked croissant, one of the many that had been dropped at their doorstep that morning from the bistro.

They'd agreed to have brunch at the Sheridan residence with the sisters, Amanda, Audrey, Grandpa Wes, and, of course, Kellan, who'd spent the night at the Sheridan house. As they approached, they heard Kellan and Audrey in the midst of a funny argument about which was better— Cinnamon Toast Crunch or Lucky Charms.

"Obviously, you like Lucky Charms because you're a teenage boy and you would prefer to take pleasure now than have regret later," Audrey said as she flipped her hair behind her shoulder. "But Cinnamon Toast Crunch is good with every single bite."

Kellan rolled his eyes. Susan realized, with a funny jump in her gut, that Kellan and Audrey would probably know one another and be friends with one another for most of their lives. That is if they both decided to stay on the island. She willed that they would.

"Look at them! The newly married couple!" Christine called from the porch as they approached.

"I can't believe you left and made us bring all the presents back here," Lola said as they stepped up. "Do you even know how much you're loved? You can probably fill that whole house up right now."

Susan stepped into the living area to assess the damage. It was true: they'd practically had to stuff the Sheridan house full of gifts from other islanders. Scott whistled. "I guess we had better get to work."

"I'm just about done making brunch," Amanda said

from the kitchen. She snapped several pancakes up into the air and then watched them ease back into the skillet.

"Hard at work, I see," Susan said as she headed over to give her daughter a hug.

"Not all of us can take a break," Amanda said as she gave her mother a huge, brilliant smile. "But I'm glad you're taking a week off of work. Me and Bruce can hold down the fort."

"I know you can," Susan said.

Grandpa Wes appeared after that. He wore a pair of binoculars around his neck and reported that he and Kellan had seen a number of summer-only species only that morning. "It's in full swing, now," he said. "Only good days ahead. Right, Kel?"

"Right," Kellan affirmed. He took several plates from the cabinet and headed out toward the picnic table to set it.

Scott squeezed Susan's hand and whispered, "I've never seen him set the table before. I wonder if he'll get it right?"

"We showed him how a week ago," Amanda announced. "The kid didn't know what he got himself into, falling into a family of mostly women. But we'll make him into a man every woman dream of— the kind who can cook, clean, set the table, and change a diaper."

"Kellan can change a diaper?" Scott asked.

"Sure can," Audrey said as she entered with Baby Max. "And he's good at it."

Scott raised his eyebrows, clearly impressed. Susan laughed. "I don't mean to corrupt your son with all this household stuff."

"No. It's a good thing," Scott said thoughtfully. "The Sheridan women are teaching him the way, just like they taught me when I was a teenager. Time has a way of repeating itself, doesn't it?"

A memory flashed through Susan's mind -- one of Anna Sheridan pressing similar plates into Scott's hands and instructing him to set the table. It seemed like something she would have done.

The family gathered around the table, just as they always had and just as they always would. Susan spoke excitedly about the inside of the Jacobson house and insisted that soon, they would all have a BBQ there to celebrate the "beginning of a new chapter." Audrey laughed and said, "Isn't a wedding supposed to be the celebration of a new chapter?" At this, Christine just shrugged and said, "The Sheridans always find new and creative ways to celebrate. You should know that by now."

The gifts were thoughtful and beautiful— a six-piece toaster, a donut-maker, new, dense towels from Paris, new robes, countless pots and pans, artwork from a local painter who'd met Susan the previous year and been "taken" with her, and so much more. There were so many that they soon recruited both Kellan and Audrey to tear open the packages.

Toward the bottom of the pile, Susan found a single card. All it read was: SUSAN, in beautiful calligraphy.

When she opened it, she found a note.

Susan,

I wasn't able to make it to your wedding because I've headed out into the world. (I hope you're reading this and that my brother managed to make the drop-off. Crossing my fingers for it, in fact.)

Probably by now, I'll be south, by a very different ocean, feeling the same sun. I'm putting the past behind me once and for all, and it's all thanks to you. I can't even begin to translate my thanks. My feelings around all of this are occasionally so monstrous, so difficult to decipher. I've turned to Rilke for some semblance of understanding.

Like this quote:

"Let everything happen to you. Beauty and terror. Just keep going. No feeling is final."

I say that to myself, over and over again. I have to believe that it's true.

I wish you endless love in your marriage. I know you deserve it. Just as we all deserve love and happiness. I'm on a quest for a new version of all of that. You've given me hope that it's possible.

All my love,
Marcie Shean

Susan pressed the letter against her chest and closed her eyes. A sharp breeze swept up from the churning waves of the Vineyard Sound; it cradled her cheek. It seemed like some kind of blessing from afar. She knew, then, that Marcie would be okay. Maybe they all would be.

Next in the series

A Vineyard Wedding

Other Books by Katie

The Vineyard Sunset Series
Secrets of Mackinac Island Series
Sisters of Edgartown Series
A Katama Bay Series
A Mount Desert Island Series
A Nantucket Sunset Series

Made in the USA
Middletown, DE
08 November 2024

64138128R00106